# THE WOMAN SHE BECAME

## BY
## LISA KIRKWOOD

# Forward

About twenty years ago, I shared my "Bus Ride from Hell" story with my manager at work. When my tale was finished, he told me I should write a book. I have toyed with that idea since then but never seemed to have the kick-start I needed to get going. The stories rolled around in my head and I knew someday I would put pen-to-paper.

One day, about six years ago, I was scrolling through my Facebook newsfeed and came across a comment someone made to a woman I know who had recently divorced her husband and posted pictures of she and her friends having fun. The comment was "so this is what you've become". Bingo! There was my inspiration. I had a title, now I just needed a story to go with it.

Although portions of the story are fiction, many were born from my own experiences as well as those of my friends and family. I have used the good and the bad; some attributed to one character and some to another.

I hope you enjoy reading as much as I have enjoyed writing. Onward now to learn all about The Woman She Became.


Lisa Kirkwood
March 2019

# PART 1

# A Girl Walked Into A Saloon

"General Store." That was the only sign on the front. The ancient oak door looked as though it could withstand a hurricane. The sun shone down onto the stained-glass window which caused the sidewalk to be ablaze with color. The image in the window was that of a wild-west saloon girl. She had a bright green plume in her hair and a black feathered boa around her neck. Her dress was a deep, blood red and the "V" of the neckline plunged scandalously low and barely covered her large breasts. The hem on one side of the dress was pulled up to the waist and revealed a long leg with a gartered stocking. The artist managed to capture the mischievousness in the woman's sapphire eyes. Her full lips were painted to match the rich red of her dress.

A girl in her early twenties jaywalked across the street and approached the store. Luckily there was no traffic because the girl's hair was hanging down into her face and blocked all peripheral vision. She stopped in front of the window and the colors, once on the sidewalk tattooed her face. She retrieved a handkerchief from her bag and wiped away the tears from her cheeks. She took a deep breath and moved forward toward the door.

The old woman watched the young girl as she entered. *'This one's got some troubles'* she whispered to no one. The girl's long blonde hair was a bit mussed and she kept pulling it slightly forward. The woman knew the girl was hiding something. A scar? Or, a bruise?

"Can I help you find something, miss?" she asked.

In a voice so small and timid the girl whispered, "Uh, um, no I'm fine." "I'm guessing that's not entirely true, child. My name is Julia. If you need anything just let me know."

Julia returned to stocking the shelves. *'A little rabbit, that's what she is'* she whispered to the can of peas in her hand. She knew the look. Unfortunately, she had seen it too many times in her life. It was the look of a defeated woman-child. Too young to realize she had the power to change her life and too old for someone else to make the change for her.

The girl wandered through the store seeming to look for everything and nothing at the same time. The store was small and only had two aisles. She made her way down the right and stopped occasionally to

pick up a can or a box, pretended to decide whether or not to but the item, then placed it back on the shelf. Because the store was so small, there was no room for a variety of brands; there were ten cans of soup on a shelf but they were all the same brand of chicken noodle. The girl was so lost within herself she did not realize she picked up a different box of the same cereal several times. She slowly walked to the front of the store and flipped through a few magazines.

"Ma'am, um, excuse me, do you have a restroom I can use?"

"Through the swingin' door at the back of the store. Bathroom's on the right."

The girl was gone for what seemed an unusually long time. Julia went to the door and tapped lightly.

"You okay in there sweetie?"

She heard the girl blow her nose then heard the water tap. The girl opened the door slowly. She ever so briefly met Julia's eyes. The girl's eyes were the strangest color of amber Julia had ever seen. In that moment, the girl's hair fell back and Julia saw there were no scars or bruises. What she saw caused her to be taken aback. This was surely one of the most beautiful faces she had ever seen.

"You're a lovely young lady, you shouldn't hide your face" Julia told her.

"You sound like my grandmother," the girl said and looked down to the floor as she walked back through the old saloon-style door.

Julia made her way slowly to the front of the store. Her feet shuffled on the ancient linoleum and made swishing sounds. Behind the counter, she had an old soda machine. There was a crisp tinkling sound as she pulled two heavy glass mugs from the shelf and began filling them.

Without turning around, she asked "Do you want vanilla syrup or a lemon?"

Startled, the girl could only stutter, "I, I. Wh-what?"

"I prefer a nice big wedge of lemon in mine" Julia continued.

Still looking at the floor, the girl whispered, "I don't have any money on me."

"I didn't ask if you wanted to *buy* one, did I? Here, I'll just make yours with vanilla. You look like you could use a little extra sweetness in your day."

Julia put both mugs on the bar and came from behind the counter.

"Sit down," she told the girl. "First of all, what's your name?"

"Marie."

"All right, Marie. You don't have to tell me anything if you don't want to, but I'm going to tell you a couple of things while we sit here."

The girl looked up slowly with what looked like fear. *'Little rabbit'*, Julia thought again.

"First off, whoever he is, he isn't worth all of this grief" Julia said.

Marie's head snapped up and there were tears formed in those not-quite-brown eyes.

"Got it on the first try, eh" Julia asked quietly.

"Maybe --," Marie choked.

"Honey, you're talkin' to an old woman. What was that saying, 'been there, done that'?" Julia grinned ever so slightly.

Marie sat stone still as one lone tear trickled down her cheek. She could not look up, she was frozen. Was it shame? Guilt? Julia could not tell. The two women, one quite old and one so very, very young just sat in silence and shipped their drinks.

"Whatever he did to you, you'll get through it, and you will heal. It's what you're going to do for yourself now that really matters."

Marie lifted her head slightly and Julia looked over just in time to see the girl roll her eyes.

"Don't look at me as though I have no clue what I'm talking about. I've already hit a nerve very hard and you know it. You've been crying

for days now, anyone can see that. Now is the time to dry those tears and move on, before you do something stupid like go back to him."

"I couldn't if I wanted to" Marie replied. "I used the last of my money to buy a bus ticket. This was as far as I could get."

"So now you feel lost. You're in this tiny town with no money, no home and no friends. That may not have been the best planning on your part, huh?"

Julia got up and returned to the soda machine to refill their glasses. As she put the fresh drinks down, she leaned on the counter, took one sun-spotted hand and reached out to gently touch the poor child's chin. She lifted slowly until Marie was forced to look at her.

"I have a small apartment upstairs. You'll stay there and you can help me around the store. When you've earned it, I'll buy you a bus ticket to go anywhere you want."

The moment she made the offer, Julia wondered just what the hell she was thinking. Generally, she was a good judge of character, but that was not always so. Lord knew she made some rash decisions when she was young. *That's EXACTLY why you're doing this you idiot – she's you forty years ago'* Julia thought as she sat back down.

"Julia? How did you end up here? Didn't you want something more than working in a little store in a tiny town?" Marie asked softly.

"Honey, I didn't *end up* here. My road to this place was long and sometimes adventurous but don't for a moment think I settled for whatever I happened upon."

Julia stood slowly and stretched her arms far above her head. The creaks and cracks of her worn joints were loud and she slowly lowered her arms and let out a long breath.

"We've got time for some story-telling tomorrow. For now, this old broad needs her rest. Come upstairs and we'll whip up something to eat. The sofa pulls out and you can sleep there. It ain't much, but it's better than the floor."

Marie stood but did not move. Julia could tell she was hesitant about staying in a stranger's home.

"Girlie," Julia said impatiently. "Where the hell else are you going to go? You gonna sit at the empty, dark bus stop and pray the boogie man doesn't come up and grab you? Pick up your damn bag and get your skinny ass upstairs."

Again, Marie was helpless to stop a crooked little grin.

"Got quite a mouth on you don't you *old lady*?"

"You ain't heard nothin' yet missy." Julia let out a haggard, dry giggle as she led the way up the back stairs. That damn giggle! She had been teased about the way she laughed for as long as she could remember. No matter how hard she tried, there was no way to stop it.

Julia awakened early. She knew without looking at the clock that it was about four in the morning. She had been waking up without the aid of an alarm clock for many, many years. She learned a long time ago how useless it was to try to go back to sleep. She never had any problem getting back into a deep slumber, but it always pissed her off when she woke up again half an hour later. It was better to just start the coffee and get going with the day.

The rich aroma of strong coffee brewing woke Marie. It took her several moments to remember where she was and why she was here. *'Damn it!'* she thought as she felt the tears well up. She squeezed her eyes closed tighter and hoped the crying would stop soon. She lie there in the dark and hoped to go back to sleep but the wonderful smell of the coffee was too pleasant to ignore. She sat up and could see Julia's small silhouette in the tiny kitchen. The only light was coming from a small children's night light on the wall at the end of the counter. A bit more alert, Marie could hear Julia sing softly.

"Good morning," Julia said without turning around. She poured a large mug of steaming coffee for each of them and sat down at the ancient Formica-topped dinette table. Marie joined her, sat quietly and stared into the swirl of creamer as she stirred her coffee. She was soon lost in those clouds. Neither of the women spoke for a long time. It seemed it should be awkward, but instead it was comforting.

Julia broke the silence and said, "I've been thinking about something. You obviously need somewhere to stay for at least a little while and I can use some help with the store. I can only pay you minimum wage, but you'll have room and board too. You stay as little or as long as you want. All I ask is that you be respectful and occasionally put up with an old woman's advice."

Marie did not answer but later followed Julia downstairs to the store and began to straighten the items on the shelves and swept the floors. The two women barely spoke throughout the day. There were few customers but each time one asked "Who's the new girl?" Julia's answer was the same. "That's Marie. She's passing through town and will be working for me until she decides what her next big adventure will be." For several days they repeated the same routine.

One evening, after closing the store, Marie asked, "Julia, just how is it you got to this place? You never answered when I asked before."

Julia's eyes twinkled. She smiled and her face beamed and was a wrinkled picture of absolute contentment. It was the face of someone who had few regrets and knew what it meant to be truly happy. She motioned with a nod toward the back of the store. "Follow me" was all she said. Julia led Marie through the swinging door, past the bathroom, stockroom and office. She opened a back door that Marie had not noticed before.

Outside was a beautiful, albeit small, garden. Marie took a deep breath and pulled in the soothing aroma of lavender. She walked around and bent to touch or smell the various plants and flowers. There were velvety roses in assorted colors. A huge grapevine covered the back wall of the yard. In the center of the garden was a small pond with fat goldfish. There was a small iron-legged table with matching chairs. Marie sat down and placed her mug on the table. Julia waited and stood just outside the door and watched Marie's reaction. Julia could not hear Marie clearly but was able to read her lips.

"It's beautiful."

Julia walked over and sat in the remaining chair. She looked at Marie and asked, "So, how did I 'end up' here? That's a pretty long tale, but here goes."

# Away From Home

Julia stood beside her packed car and looked up to her mother standing on the front porch. Try as she might, her mother could not hide the worried look.

"Mom, I'll be fine. I have my maps, I have plenty of water and I have my list of phone numbers."

Her mother walked toward her and reached out to cup Julia's face in her hands. For a moment, she saw the tiny little girl with ratty pigtails and skinned knees.

"Pay attention to any road closure signs. I don't want you getting stuck. Your dad marked alternate routes on your map. Make sure you call every time you stop."

"I promise. I love you, Mom."

"Love you too, sweetie."

Julia turned to walk down the driveway but stopped to look back at the house that held so many fond memories. Her mother fumbled nervously with the belt of her robe and tried to not cry.

"This is a good thing, Mom," she said. She took one last peek at the house as she backed out of the driveway, waved to her mother and drove away from home. The road ahead was unknown and that scared her; but it excited her as well. Once she was away from the chaos of the dense Atlanta traffic, she found a classic rock station on the radio and cranked up the volume. As she left her beloved city behind, Julia thought of her best friend Anna.

*Julia and her best friend Anna are, for the most part, inseparable during their high school years. So often are they seen together, the other kids and even some of the teachers, began calling the two Julianna. They talk about all the things teenage girls do; boys, their parents, which girl has a crush on which boy at school. They listen to music for hours while experimenting with make-up and hairdos. They spend every Friday night at the mall or at the school's football game and, until they are old enough to drive, every Saturday night is spent at the skating rink. When they are old enough to begin dating, they are usually found as a group of four. The closeness of the*

*friendship is well known, so any boy that decides to go out with one knows he will essentially be dating the other as well.*

*The teenaged team of Julianna is, as usual, trolling for boys at the mall. Generally, they will meet up with boys their own age. Bored with the goofiness and lack of maturity of these young lads, the girls decide to set their sights on the more 'advanced' boys. Leaning over the rail of the upper level looking down onto the food court of the mall, Anna spots two promising boys. With her elbow Anna nudges Julia and yells down to these strapping young specimens. Each girl is quite beautiful; more so than either would ever imagine, and getting the attention of hormone-driven males is never a problem. The girls smile to each other and begin discussing which one they want as the boys head toward the escalator. Surprisingly, they rarely want the same boy. Although their tastes are quite similar, they seem to never fight over boys. Equally amazing is how the boy one of the girls picks always approaches that girl first, appearing to ignore the other girl. Introductions are quickly made. Jerry and Zack are freshmen at the local engineering college. Julia and Anna announce they are also freshman, although they omit the very important fact that they are still in high school. Soon, the two new couples are walking through the mall hand-in-hand. The girls are still naïve enough to think this short time is the 'getting to know you' stage and, thinking they know who these young men are, follow them to the mall parking lot. Anna and Jerry get into the back seat of the car and begin kissing. Starting to feel apprehensive about leaving the security of the mall, Julia just sits staring out the window. She tries hard to appear bored but, in truth, she is watching for customers going to and from their cars or for mall security on patrol. Zack leans over to turn on the radio for which Julia is thankful. The smacking and grunting from the back seat is beyond sickening now and Julia just wants to leave. Julia's silent prayers are answered when a golf cart marked "SECURITY" pulls up next to the car. The rotund guard walks over and taps on the back window. Anna sits up quickly, her hair is a mess and her mascara is smeared. With their heads hanging in shame and embarrassment the girls walk quickly back to the mall. Neither speaks until they are in the restroom.*

*"That was pretty dumb of us you know," Julia says to Anna's reflected image in the mirror. "What if they had just decided to drive off?" she continues.*

*Turning to face Julia, Anna shrugs her shoulders and replies, "then we'd have to kick their asses."*

*As Anna strides out of the bathroom, Julia rolls her eyes and shouts, "You're crazy! You know that don't you?"*

*Julia takes a few extra moments at the sink splashing cold water on her face. It is not until this moment the full impact of what might have happened hit her and she is momentarily frozen with fear.*

*Looking up to her reflection in the mirror, she whispers, "Don't you do something that goddam stupid again. EVER!"*

"Aw, fuck it!" Julia blurts as she kicks off her shoes revealing toenails painted a sparkly electric blue. This she did just as the girl ahead of her is called to the stage. The girl turns and looks at Julia with surprise and disgust.

Julia tries to whisper but it comes out louder than she intends, "What the hell are you looking at? Go on; perform for your captive audience."

Flustered, the girl almost trips over the hem of her gown and her face flushes red with embarrassment.

"Remember to smile pretty," Julia teases.

Waiting for her turn, Julia begins quietly repeating "Waiting in the wings. Waiting in the wings. Waiting in the wings." Just as her name is called, the recitation changes to "Wading in the wings." Walking barefoot onto the stage, she suddenly has an image of herself in a pool of Buffalo wings; sauce clinging to her hair and running down her arms. As she reaches the middle of the stage, she erupts with laughter. Being a carefree person who is unafraid to play to the fool, she decides to give into her own silliness and begins to dance up the runway. She turns at the end of the runway, gives a little shake of her rear end and starts toward the main stage. She reaches down and grabs her dress just above the knees, lifting it up so she can move more freely. Her knees are scratched and bruised from a fall while running and are quite a comical contrast to the onyx-beaded gown. She turns quickly to fac the audience, throws her arms open wide and takes and exaggerated bow.

"Now that was fun!" she announces to the people staring at her. It is easy to pick out the mothers of the girls that take this seriously; they all look as though they smell something rotten. Many of the men and boys in the crowd are trying to conceal their wide smiles.

Walking over to stand by Anna, Julia leans over and whispers, "How the hell did I let you talk me into this? A damn be-yoo-tee-pageant?"


The remining high school years go by quickly. It is during these years Julia experiences many of her 'firsts'. She falls in love, loses her virginity, suffers heartache when the relationship inevitably ends. She gets drunk for the first time and tries her

best to hide from her mother the hangover she suffers as a result. She is caught trying to spend the night with a boy when his parents are out of town.

Throughout these years, Julia and Anna remain the closest of friends. The girls know this will change soon, no matter how much they wish to be best friends forever. Graduation is quickly approaching and Anna will be leaving for college in the fall. Never an attentive student, Julia decides against continuing her education and begins looking for a job. Knowing their time together will soon come to an end, the girls spend as much time together as they can that summer. As the weather stars to cool, the girls feel a sadness blanket them. Julia spends the night at Anna's house the night before Anna leaves for school. Awaking early the next morning, the girls load Anna's car and begin their goodbyes. Although she manages to remain dry-eyed and stoic during the hugs and promises to stay in touch, Julia can feel the crushing weight of how much she will miss her friend. Moments after Anna's car clears the end of the driveway, Julia begins walking to her own car. Once inside, she sits quietly for a few minutes then starts the ignition. The song on the radio is one Julia and Anna love and play frequently. Silently at first, Julia begins to cry; first a lone tear then a waterfall. Sitting in her car with her tear-streaked face buried in her hands, she does not see the older woman approach the car. Anna's mother lightly taps on the window. Startled, Julia jumps and cries harder when she sees who is standing there. She gets out of the car and the woman she thinks of as her surrogate mother wraps her arms around the young girl and holds her until the sobs cease. Anna's mother gently holds Julia's shoulders, pushes her back slightly and gives her a kiss on the forehead.

Softly she says, "It's all part of the growing up sweetie."

Julia gets back into her car and heads home. As she drives away from Anna's house, she looks into the rearview mirror and whispers, "Goodbye Julianna."

She arrived in beautiful Savannah and was overcome by the sight of the stately trees shrouded in Spanish moss. She stopped first at Forsyth Park. She followed the pathway and arrived at the north end of the park and sat on a bench near the fountain. She closed her eyes and appeared to be meditating. She listed to the water spurt from the cherub-like figures that surround the center of the fountain. She could hear the many birds call to each other from one massive oak to another and the bees that buzzed in the numerous azalea bushes. She was consumed by the lush grounds and, although there were quite a few people walking through the park, Julia was oblivious to their presence. So enthralled was she that measured time seemed to be nonexistent. The gnawing gurgle of her stomach brought her back to reality.

She left the park and found her way to The Pirate's House. A block from the Savannah River, the building was once an inn used by seaman to rest, drink and relax before heading back out to sea. Hung on a wall inside were framed pages from an early and rare edition of Treasure Island. Legend had it that Captain Flint died in one of the rooms upstairs. Julia entered one of the dining rooms. Massive beamed ceilings hung far above the small tables covered in red and white checked tablecloths with crisp, white napkins tented at each setting. The wall of exposed, sturdy brick was covered in framed paintings. Unable to choose any one item from the variety of menu offerings, she decided to get something then for lunch and order something to go for dinner that night. She ordered the catfish basket and a bowl of She Crab soup which consisted of crabmeat, brandy and cream. Although she opened a book to read, she never made it past the first sentence. The atmosphere of the restaurant was too intriguing and she stared at the décor and structural design of the historic building. She received her take out order of grilled salmon Caesar salad and a bowl of okra gumbo and, reluctantly, left the fascinating restaurant and museum.

With several hours left before dark, Julia decided to take a walk along the Savannah River. She sat down on the brick wall and watched the life around the river, as well as the life the river itself seemed to have. She looked down the river and could just make out the red and white riverboat as it carried passengers along. Since she grew up in the busy metropolitan area of Atlanta, she was not used to the relaxed and easy way people in Savannah appeared to be. In the short time she had been there, she decided a simpler life had its merits and vowed that one day she would live in a place this peaceful.

The sun had begun its decent and Julia knew it was time to leave. For a moment, the serenity was forgotten when she reflected on why she was making this trip. Her aunt lived in a small coastal town in South Carolina and the town had recently been damaged by a hurricane. Julia would be staying with her aunt while she helped with the cleanup and rebuilding of the stricken neighborhood. She drove away from Savannah and, as she did, she looked in the rearview mirror to catch one last look at the historic town. It began to glow with the red-orange fire of the setting sun.

Having arrived after the sun disappeared for the night, Julia had not been able to see clearly the damage caused by the powerful storm. When she awoke the next morning, she looked out of the upstairs bedroom window and saw only a portion of the destruction. A neighbor only a few houses away had a huge hole in the roof of the garage and large support beams had crushed the tiny compact car parked there. Just over the top of the house directly across the street she saw the canted roof of the house on the next block. Without being able to see the entire house, Julia assumed it was just the roof that sustained the damage; she later learned the entire foundation of the house had moved fifteen feet into what was once a driveway. She turned from the window and began looking through the clothes she had unpacked the night before. There was a cool breeze blowing through the window but she knew the day would turn humid soon. She chose some light-weight jeans, a tank top and one of her father's old button-down oxford shirts and walked to the bathroom to shower. As she dried off, she smelled the wonderful aroma of bacon. She walked down the stairs and pulled her long blonde hair into a ponytail as she went. She checked her reflection in the hall mirror, gave herself a shrug of the shoulders and a grin and strode into the kitchen. Her eyes grew large at the sight before her and she looked in disbelief at her aunt.

"All of this isn't for just *us*, is it?" Julia asked.

"Good Lord, no!" replied Virginia. "We wouldn't be able to move for days if we ate all of this. My kitchen is the home base so to speak. Each morning all of the volunteers get a hearty breakfast and their assignments for the day."

Laid out on the table were platters of food. There were stacks of steaming, fluffy pancakes and waffles, sausages in links and patties, thick cut bacon, scrambled as well as fried eggs. She saw at least three different kind of cheese, a mound of biscuits as well as white and wheat toast. In the center of the table was a punch

bowl full of gravy.  A small side table held pitchers of grape, orange and apple juice and a pot of hot coffee.  A small cooler had both regular milk and buttermilk packed in ice.

"Aunt Ginny, I would have helped.  Why didn't you wake me up?" Julia asked.

"Good grief!  I didn't make all of this by myself" Virginia said laughingly.  "The other ladies dropped off their contributions just a little bit ago.  Grab a bowl from the cabinet and pour those grits into it and find a place on the table, would you, dear?" Virginia asked.

Julia placed a stack of plates on a card table in one corner.  Her aunt handed her a large box that contained hundreds of plastic spoons, forks and knives, then piled two sleeves of Styrofoam cups on top of the box.  Julia approached the small table and caught her foot on the leg of a chair that had been pulled out.  The cups flew from the box and bounced onto the floor.  Julia fell forward, landing on top of the box then rolled sideways landing on her back on the tile floor.  It was not until then she noticed the handsome young man standing in the doorway of the kitchen.  Although she had certainly blushed before, Julia could not recall her cheeks ever feeling so hot and tingly.  For what may have been the first time in her life, Julia was speechless and shy.  His hair was very short and looked as though it might be a dark blonde when longer.  He had broad, muscular shoulders and she could see the perfectly toned thighs through his tight blue jeans.  Bending over her, he reached out to pick up the box.  Until then Julia had not realized she was still holding it by the cutout handles.  Casually holding the box in one hand, he extended the other to Julia and she absently lifted her arm and put her tiny hand in his.  His palms were calloused but surprisingly smooth and it was obvious he had no problem working hard.  His brilliant emerald green eyes sparkled and, when he smiled, Julia wondered if she would have the strength to stand.  Effortlessly, he helped her up and placed the box on the table.  Reaching out, he brushed a lock of hair out of her eyes.  She was helpless to do anything but stare.

"Gotta watch out for those chairs," he said.  He leaned toward her slightly and whispered, "I've seen them jump out at people before, but I don't think I ever saw one actually get somebody."

Julia burst out laughing and managed to find the chair just in time as she sat down hard. Still laughing, she buried her face in her hands.

"I cannot believe I did that," she said as she tilted her head up toward him and rolled her eyes.

It was not until then that Julia noticed her aunt walking around the large table in the adjacent dining room obviously trying not to look or laugh. Julia found strength in her legs and stood up. She reached out her hand.

"My name is Julia," she said as he took her hand in a firm handshake. "I'm Virginia's niece."

"Nice to meet you Julia. My name is Sam. My grandparents live next door. I'm here from Wyoming for my annual summer visit with them."

"I guess I'd better help Virginia. It sounds like people are starting to arrive. I'll see you later, Sam."

"See you, klutz," Sam said with a wide grin.

It seemed as though hundreds of people had been through the house that morning. Julia looked at the once overflowing table and saw that the only food left was a small, broken piece of bacon and a few slices of cheese with the edges starting to curl. Virginia slowly walked back into the kitchen, having just said goodbye to the last group. She sat down slowly and reached over to take the tiny bit of bacon and popped it into her mouth.

"Please tell me you don't do this *every* morning Aunt Ginny," Julia said as she looked upon the exhausted woman.

"It's only like this on the first day. Unfortunately, we lose most of the volunteers after a day or two. Either they can't be away from home very long, or the work is more than they anticipated and they just don't come back. Tomorrow they will go to someone else's house. We have about ten of us that rotate breakfast duty and we switch who gets the first morning. Thanks for all of your help. I'm not sure I can do First Morning anymore." Virginia took a sideways look toward Julia and said quietly, "I'm just gettin' too damn old."

A large yellow cat cautiously walked in the kitchen and rubbed itself against Virginia's leg.

"I had a cat like him when I was little," Julia said as she reached down to scratch the feline behind the ears.

*The little girl runs around in the sunbaked yard, her long, golden hair flowing in waves behind her. Her mother sits on the front porch steps enjoying the vitality and complete innocence exuding from her daughter. A gargantuan, yellow tabby chases the little girl. It leaps up to catch the curly locks of the girl's hair and knocks her to the ground. The moment the cat lets go, the girl squeals and jumps up and starts running again. The tiny giggles are so soft and sweet. The sound bounces off of the side of the house then disappears into the sweltering Texas gloaming. The game of tag continues for what seems ages but the sun will be disappearing soon and it is dinner time.*

*"Come on, Julia. You can play with Kitty again tomorrow," the mother says.*

*With her shoulders slumped and a tangled mess of blonde hair hiding her face, Julia tromps up the stairs. She has coarse, dead*

*grass in her hair, identically skinned knees and there is a smudge of dirt across her tiny forehead.  The woman places a tender kiss on top of the little one's head and places her hand on the child's back to guide her back inside.*

Julia spent the rest of the morning helping Virginia clean up. When they were finished, she decided to walk around the neighborhood. The numerous volunteers had already managed to clear the large trees that had fallen, or were uprooted, and they started to remove the debris from the yards. Julia looked around and was amazed that no one in the town was seriously injured. She knew from her aunt that a few people had broken bones and an old man a few streets over suffered a heart attack, but he survived and was improving. A few blocks from her aunt's house, she recognized Sam in a crowd of men in front of a house and stopped to say hello. They had been wrapping a chain around an amazingly large tree trunk to drag it away. Sam excused himself from the group when he saw Julia approach. The two young people talked for a few minutes and Julia nervously invited Sam to Virginia's house that evening for dinner. The group of volunteers walked back to the large tree and Julia realized she had probably taken too much of Sam's time and said goodbye. As she walked away, she could hear some of the men tease Sam. She tried to make sure it was not noticeable when she walked a little bit faster. She knew the sooner she was out of sight, the sooner the men would leave Sam alone.

It was several hours before dinner-time and Julia decided to go to the beach for a while. Although she did not know the neighborhood well, she was able to follow the sounds of the waves crashing along the shore. Several blocks later she caught glimpses of the ocean between the houses. She found a yard with no fence and hoped the owners would not mind if she used their property as a shortcut. As she rounded the corner of the house, a large black and tan dog charged toward her. His teeth were bared in a menacing snarl and he barked viciously. Julia stood frozen and when the dog began a barreling leap toward her, the chain attached to his collar was snapped taut and pulled him back to the ground. An older man opened the screen door and called to the dog. Julia looked at him and he saw the terror in her eyes.

The man grinned and said, "Guess you know now why I don't bother putting up a fence."

Julia apologized profusely and headed back to the street. The dog jumped to all four feet and gave one final bark; he knew he had done his job and protected his master. Julia walked further down the street until she saw a sidewalk that led to the public entrance of the beach. It was not until she bent over to remove her shoes that she realized how badly she had been shaking. She usually had no fear of dogs, even large ones, but something about the eyes

of this one had affected her more than she would have thought possible.  She inhaled the sea air deep into her lungs and let out an audible sigh.  She envisioned pushing the terror from her body.  She closed her eyes and absorbed the sound and smell of the ocean and soon had the image of the charging dog erased from her mind.  She let out another long-held breath, opened her eyes and allowed the picturesque scene to envelope her.  She concentrated on the roar of the waves and the call of the gulls that flew overhead.  She walked toward the water, and noticed the debris left behind from the storm.  It dawned on her then that, with so many volunteers working to repair the homes and streets, there was not much time to clear the beach.  She decided she would ask Virginia if anyone had formed a beach cleanup group.  She looked toward the sky and realized it was late and that she needed to head back to the house.  She enjoyed the solitude and decided to walk along the beach in the general direction of her aunt's street.  She hoped there would be another sidewalk that led back to the neighborhood.  For just a moment the vision of the dog came back but Julia pushed it back quickly.

She primarily watched the tide come in as she walked, but occasionally looked inland to the houses along the beach.  She saw a recently cleared lot with a bulldozer sitting to one side and piles of wood to the other.  In the center of the yard was an old mobile home.  The house had sustained too much damage in the storm and had been leveled instead of attempting repairs.  The trailer looked to be about eight feet off of the ground and appeared to be temporary until the owners could rebuild.  She heard a loud cracking sound and looked up just in time to see the floor of the trailer fall.  What she saw next initially confused her but then she began to laugh hysterically.  Where only moments before was empty space, a family sat in a large bathtub.  Still laughing uncontrollably, she ran up the small hill toward them.  The father climbed out of the tub just as Julia approached and she was quite thankful to see they all had bathing suits on.

"Are you guys okay?  What happened?" Julia managed to ask through the chuckles.

The mother took the hand Julia had extended to help her up.

"We went to the beach and got in the bath together to rinse off the sand.  Just as we were starting to dry off, we fell through the floor."

With the initial shock of crashing through the floor faded, the little girl began to cry. The mother leaned over and picked up the small child to comfort her.

"You're not hurt sweetie, you just got a bit of a jolt that's all," the mother said quietly to the girl.

Not wanting the little one to think she was being laughed at, Julia turned her head slightly and pretended to look toward the water. When she was able to compose herself, she turned back to the stunned family.

"You're sure none of you are hurt?" she asked the father.

"We're good. Thank you for running up to check on us," he said.

"Do you have somewhere else you can stay?" Julia inquired. "You can't possibly stay here tonight."

"My sister lives a couple of doors down, we can spend the night with her and we'll figure out something else tomorrow," the mother replied.

Unable to completely hide the smile that crept across her face, Julia said "Alright, if you're sure."

The trio walked up the steps and re-entered the trailer. As she began her trek back to the beach, Julia was amazed how resilient people could be. This family had just lost two homes in just as many weeks, yet they were casually chatting and laughing when they closed the front door.

Daylight began to fade and Julia hoped she could find her way back to Virginia's house before darkness fell. She started to think she should not have wandered so far away. The image of the wide-eyed, shocked expressions on the faces of the small family brought on a giggle that turned into a full belly laugh. Julia tried to imagine what she must look like to anyone looking out toward the beach.

"Like a lunatic, that's what," she said to a sea gull hopping around in the sand. The gull looked at Julia and cried out. "Great, now I'm having a conversation with a bird!" she said as she broke into a fresh fit of giggles.

She managed to find her way back to the house and arrived just as the skies began turning red from the setting sun. She approached the front door and heard voices inside. Although she had only spoken to him a few times, she immediately recognized Sam's soothing baritone voice. She had forgotten about her invitation and had not arrived home in time to let her aunt know they would have company. She walked into the kitchen where Virginia and Sam sat at the dining table enjoying cold beers. Virginia turned around and rested her elbow on the back of the chair and gave Julia a look. It was not quite a reprimand, but the look conveyed she was not happy about not being told someone would come by. The glare quickly faded and Julia saw a slight glimmer in the woman's eyes and the corners of her mouth lifted slightly into a knowing grin.

"About time you got here. Where the heck did you go all afternoon?" Virginia asked.

"I'm sorry, Aunt Ginny. I would have been here much sooner but I was walking along the beach, and I had to make sure the family was okay," Julia stammered.

Virginia and Sam stared at Julia with questions in their eyes. She realized she was not making sense to either of them. She told the story and soon all three of them were laughing. Virginia got up and got another beer from the refrigerator and wiped tears from the corners of her eyes.

"I'll have to call them tomorrow to see if they need anything. I'm glad no one was hurt," Virginia said. "Now, we've got to decide what we're going to feed this young man."

Dinner was eaten and the kitchen was cleaned up. Sam and Julia went outside and sat in the swing on the front porch. They chatted casually and watched the moon as it began to cross the night sky. Sam talked of his childhood riding bikes and playing football. Although she was listening, Julia had a somewhat distant look in her eyes.

*She sits on the bicycle at the top of the hill. The group of boys around her begin to goad her.*

*"You'll never do it."*

*"Chicken."*

*"Betcha can't."*

*She is scared but refuses to let the boys see it. Julia is nervous because she is going to ride Vince's bike. She has quite a crush on him. He is the real reason she has accepted the boys' challenge; she is showing off and trying to impress Vince. 'You can do this. Just show them.' She is unable to withstand their taunts any longer. The greatest trick will be the quick lane change when she leaves the sidewalk and starts down the second hill. She lets the bike roll a few feet then starts pedaling as fast as she can. She is off of the sidewalk in smoothest fashion. Faster and faster her legs pump. The small hill she is supposed to jump is coming up quickly. Too quickly. She can feel a loss of control and decides too late that she is not going to make it. She tries to back pedal to engage the brake but nothing happens. She has just ridden through a large patch of late summer clover and it is wet from the rain this afternoon. The tires are slick and the brake pad is unable to grab the rubber of the tire. That is the last thing Julia remembers. The rest is lost. The next thing she is aware of is lying in the back of the station wagon with a bowl next to her head. Looking up she can see her little sister hanging over the back seat, staring wide-eyed and looking quite sacred. She fades again and the next thing she remembers is waking up at home. She is on a make-shift bed in the middle of the living room floor. Her arms are wrapped in bandages and she tries hard to remember what happened.*

*The next morning there is a light knock at the front door. "Julia, your friends would like to see you," her mother says as she opens the door to let the boys inside.*

*The three of them stand in the doorway and seem to have lost the ability to speak. Gone are the teasing and the dares. Now they are just scared little boys who do not know what to do or say.*

*In a voice barely audible, Vince says, "I'm sorry you got hurt. Hope you feel better soon." He looks up at Julia's mother and mumbles, "Sorry."*

*He and the other boys leave, shuffling their feet as though their legs are made of stone.*

*For as long as she lives, Julia will never have any memory of the accident; although there are stories galore. Ben tells everyone he saved Julia's life because he ran to get his father. Brian tells anyone that will listen that Vince ran down the hill yelling 'Look what she did to my bike' and that Vince did not care one bit about some dumb girl. Although she has no way to know if any part of it is true, throughout her life Julia will tell of the event as she has heard it from the boys.*

*When the brakes failed, she hit the first hill too fast and did two back flips in the air and landed on the front tire. She then spun 360 degrees and hit the ground. Her wrists were fractured when she tried to break her fall and her face slammed into the mud, pulling her bottom lip as she slid. In the years to come, she will joke that she was the first extreme sports athlete and that it is such as shame there was no record of it on film.*

*The accident is the advent of Julia's tomboy ways. She is back on a bike with both arms in plaster casts. She learns to do handstands and cartwheels on her fists instead of the flat palm of her hand. She discovers the casts can be used as weapons when a boy in the neighborhood keeps pestering her. She would rather play football, ride bikes, ride skateboards or run than play with anything girly. The Barbie dolls she occasionally receives as gifts are used as rockets to launch from the top of the hill. The rich, red Georgia clay makes great dirt bombs, which are then used as ammunition during games of king of the hill.*

Absently she made a comment about performing stunts on a bicycle. Sam gave her a curious look and Julia told him of her one day as a daredevil rider. When she was finished telling the story, her mind once again drifted back to her childhood.

*Julia loves to run and it is quite common for her to accept gladly the racing challenges from the boys. She has long, strong legs and usually wins. She attempts other organized sports but seems to lack talent and finesse for most of them. In softball, she never seems to get a hit and mostly misses any ball hit in her direction. In volleyball, she always seems to be in someone's way.*

*Julia discovers she loves playing football. She has a respectable throwing arm and generally catches passes thrown to her. Since she can outrun most of the boys, she has little difficulty scoring touchdowns and she is a decent kicker.*

*When she is twelve, she plays what is supposed to be a game of touch football and one of the older boys tackles her. He seems to be taking a long time getting up and Julia is telling him to get off of her. About the time he says, "I won't have any problem getting off," Julia realizes she can feel his erection on the back of her leg. She manages to wiggle out from under him and get up. With her face a blazing red and her blonde hair full of dried leaves and grass, she bends down and looks him in the eye. Her usually kind eyes turn a darker blue and the boy sees for the first time what people mean when they talk of a look shooting flames.*

*Julia hisses, "Don't you ever come near me again, asshole!"*

*There will be times through the years she regrets not punching him in the nose while he was down. Other times, she is proud that she walked away holding her head high.*

Julia and Sam spent their days helping with the clean-up and rebuilding efforts. Evenings were usually spent sitting in the front porch swing or walking on the beach. As the weeks went by, they were seen together more and more. The old people would whisper as the young couple passed. Most of the community had known Sam since he was a small boy, visiting his grandparents in the summer. Although Julia was a newcomer, the folks knew her aunt very well. Having proven herself to be hard working and joyous to be near, the young woman quickly became accepted into their neighborhood. While sitting on the beach one evening, Sam and Julia casually talked about the lack of privacy they had in the small town. Sam suggested they take a short road trip and get away for a few days. They decided to drive north toward Myrtle Beach.

They took a long route that led them further inland so that they could avoid the heavier tourist traffic. With no particular plan, they stayed to the smaller roads so they could drive slower and take in the scenery of the tiny communities. They were close to Fort Sumter and decided to take a tour of the old structure. Julia walked up to a large cannon and placed her hand on the side. She tried to imagine how deafening the sound must have been when it was fired. She wondered how the brick of the building withstood the reverberations emitted from this large weapon. Although there were some areas that had begun to crumble, Julia was amazed the building held up as well as it had through the many, many years.

They stayed the night at a small hotel near Fort Sumter. They awoke early the next morning and began the drive eastward. They realized they were hungry and decided to stop in a tiny community that had a restaurant and a park. The day was warm but the humidity was low and they decided to eat outside. Across the park was a small church and they watched as the people arrived for services. All of the doors and windows were open and Sam and Julia heard the voices as the people sang joyously. Later, they heard as the preacher began. Individual words were difficult to distinguish as they floated across the park but there was no mistaking the passionate, imploring tone. Sam noticed Julia had a small grin that crept across her face.

Julia is sitting with her family in church. It is a beautiful Georgia autumn day. The wind is crisp and the leaves are an explosion of red and gold. Julia wants more than anything to get outside and play. The lace of her pretty canary-yellow dress is stiff and scratches her legs. She is growing increasingly restless in the pew. She begins tearing the bulletin into tiny pieces; unaware she has been dropping them to the floor. She eventually realizes what she has been doing and sees she made quite a mess. She slides from her seat to begin picking up the bits of paper. Her mother lightly taps her on the shoulder and motions for Julia to sit back down and mouths one word 'Later'. She knows she should be sitting still, listening to the preacher but, if she looks at him she will start to laugh. His face is red and Julia can see the veins popping out on his neck. She wonders, if God loves us and we are supposed to be kind to one another, why does this man always seem to be so angry? Deciding he might be mad at her for all of the fidgeting, she tries very hard to be still.

She is unaware she is falling asleep until she hears the organist start the hymn. She recognizes the song and knows this signals the end of the service. She also knows it could be eons before they can leave. Unless someone goes to the altar to pray soon, they will have to sit through endless stanzas of 'Just As I Am'. Julia decides, this time, she will make sure they get home soon. Ever so slowly, she stands up and makes her way past the other parishioners on her row, whispering "Excuse me," as she tries not to step on their feet. With great care, she begins the long walk up the aisle to the front of the church. She watches the deep red carpet intently, wanting to make sure she does not make eye contact with the reverend. She kneels down, clasps her small hands together, places them under her chin and bows her head. Her golden ringlets fall forward hiding her face. Slowly, making sure no one can see, she starts pulling the hairs inside her nose. She cannot remember where she learned this trick, but many of her friends do it when they want sympathy from teachers or parents. Soon her eyes begin to water. She allows time for the congregation to sing one verse. She tugs the hairs once more and gives a quick, but hard, bite to her tongue. The tears spill over her long eyelashes. She slowly raises her head and meets the preacher's gaze long enough for him to see rosy tear-streaked cheeks. 'Amen' and 'Hallelujah' can be heard from the congregation. Julia is smiling, having just invited Jesus into her life, or so the others believe. There are hugs and kisses from the old ladies and pats on the head from the old men. She is the only one that knows her mischievous grin is pride in what she has just

*been able to accomplish. All of the grown-ups would sit for half an hour waiting for the minister to give the benediction, but a little girl has fooled them all and now everyone gets to go home. With her head held high, and her chest puffed out, she makes her way back to her parents. She is quite proud of herself until she sees her mother's face. She knows that look. The lips are so thin they have almost disappeared and Julia would swear there were actual bolts of lightning shooting from her mother's eyes. She has not fooled everyone. She expects quite a tongue-lashing but what happens instead is almost more frightening. Her mother does not say a single word.*

*That night, as Julia is getting ready for bed, her mother peeks into the room and says, "I love you. Goodnight. Maybe you should go ahead and say your prayers and ask for forgiveness for the little stunt you pulled in church today." She gently closes the door, leaving Julia standing in the middle of her room, stunned.*

*Julia uttered the first bad word of her young life, "Well, shit!" and plopped face-down on her bed.*

Sam asked Julia what she was thinking about and she told him. Julia finished recounting her story and they realized the pleading shouts of the preacher had lowered in volume. As if on cue, the sound of the organ filled the air. Sam and Julia started to laugh when they recognize the song and the congregation began to sing 'Just As I Am".

The hard work of the volunteers paid off. Repairs had been completed on the less damaged homes and businesses. Foundation and framing were finished for the houses that had to be torn down and rebuilt. The nights were becoming slightly cooler and the humidity was lessening. Try as she might, Julia was unable to completely hide the melancholy feeling that crept in. Sam was only visiting to help the town and to visit with his grandparents. Julia reminded herself over and over that she knew going in that this would only be a summer romance but it did not rid the sadness she began to feel. Although he did not talk of it openly, she could tell that Sam was feeling the same. They continued to spend each evening together and would sneak off for private moments as much as possible.

The evening before Sam planned to leave, he arranged to stay at a small home on a tiny island nearby. The owner was a family friend who was on vacation with his children. Earlier in the day, Virginia helped Sam plan a romantic dinner for he and Julia to share. He picked up Julia and they drove across the small bridge that led to the island. A small, sandy path, barely wide enough for a vehicle, cut through the dense trees. The path opened to a small yard and the cottage-style home came into view. Julia stepped out of the car and noticed that the only sounds were the distant waves and various birds in the trees. Cut off from the noises of town activities, a deep serenity surrounded the home. Sam led Julia through the front door. The home was tastefully decorated and the walls were covered with framed candid photos of a life well-lived and enjoyed. It was small and somehow felt comfortably full without being overcrowded. A large fireplace was the central feature in the cozy living room. The kitchen was proportioned to the rest of the space but a large window gave the illusion of a much larger area. Sam left Julia to roam around the house while he went to the refrigerator to retrieve a bottle of wine. He hoped she would not look out onto the back porch; he wanted to be with her when his surprise was revealed. His worry was unfounded. When he returned from the kitchen, Julia was standing in the hallway admiring more of the family photos. He tucked the bottle of wine under his arm, held the two glasses in one hand and took Julia's hand with the other. He led her out of the house to the backyard. A large deck stretched the length of the house and continued around a corner leading to a small area with an outdoor fireplace. A table dressed with a linen cloth and candles awaited the couple. Sam lit the fireplace and poured the wine. He handed Julia her glass then reached for a small remote control on the table. Soft music surrounded them. Sam pulled Julia close and began to sway slowly in perfect cadence with the

soft beat of the music. Julia closed her eyes, laid her head in the hollow between Sam's neck and shoulder, and allowed herself to become lost in the precious moment. They danced for several songs and Sam hummed along with the music. Julia could feel the vibrations of his throat against her forehead. Reluctantly, Sam pulled away and went into the house. Leaning slightly on the railing of the porch, Julia looked west to watch the setting sun. Beautiful shades of orange and pink grew deeper as the sun disappeared. Sam came out of the house precariously balancing two plates in one arm and an ice bucket with a second bottle of wine tucked under the other. Julia stepped quickly toward him when she saw one of the plates rock slightly when Sam used his foot to shut the door. She managed to grab both plates just before they tipped and she carried them to the table. Sam lit the candles which shone brighter as the sky darkened. The soft glow illuminated their faces and each could see the sadness in the other's eyes. They ate slowly and chatted quietly wanting to savor this moment. When they finished eating, Sam opened the other bottle of wine and poured them each a fresh glass. Sam walked around the corner and flipped a switch. Tiny lights twinkled above the couple and they danced again. Julia had begun to feel warm as the wine washed through. Sam kissed her neck; the mild warmth changed quickly to an intense heat. Sam took the glass from Julia's hand, blew out the candles and led her through the French door into the bedroom.

Sam woke the next morning to the smells of coffee and bacon. It was still dark outside but he saw the faintest beginning of dawn. Quietly he walked into the kitchen. Julia stood at the stove. Her hair was pulled into a messy ponytail and she wore only his shirt from the night before. She heard him approaching but continued to cook.

"If you're trying to sneak up on me, you're doing a shitty job you know," she said teasingly.

He walked up behind her and wrapped his arms around her waist and bumped the back of his hand on the hot pan. He looked over her shoulder and saw she was stirring thick, white gravy with large chunks of sausage. It was not until then he noticed the smell of biscuits.

"You gonna share any of that?" he whispered in her ear.

"Maybe," she said, then turned around to give him a light kiss.

Sam poured them each a steaming cup of coffee and got plates and silverware. Julia quickly scrambled some eggs and sprinkled them with shredded cheese. Not a shy eater, Julia loaded her plate almost as much as Sam did his. It was not until he was nearly finished that he spoke.

"I didn't realize how hungry I was until I started eating. I think I may have to go back for more," Sam said around another mouthful of food. "Is everything you cook this good?"

"Probably not everything. You have to understand though; my Southern Women's membership card would be revoked if I couldn't make breakfast," she replied.

"Your what?"

"Didn't you know? It's mandatory for any good Southern woman to make certain things very well. Biscuits and gravy, grits, fried chicken, pot roast and potato salad," she said, holding up her hand and tapping a finger for each item. "If you can't accomplish at least these basics, you're not allowed in the club," she said using her best Southern drawl.

Sam and Julia cleaned up the kitchen and went out to the porch to drink their coffee and watch as the day began. Julia leaned her head back against the chair and quietly sat and listened to the birds. Looking toward Julia, Sam noticed a tiny tear in the corner of her eye.

"You okay?" he asked.

She raised her head slowly and turned to look at him. She took a moment to compose herself and took down her ponytail then re-tied it.

"I promised myself I wouldn't cry," she said in a small, choked voice.

Sam got up from his chair and walked over to Julia. He reached out his hand and, when she took it, he silently led her back into the house. Cupping her tear-streaked face in his hands, he kissed her forehead gently.

"I guess we've both been trying our damnedest to ignore the fact this day was coming," he said to her in a lover's husky voice.

They spent the rest of the morning in the bedroom until they could no longer ignore the inevitable. Suffering a combination of exhaustion from their lovemaking as well as the sorrow they were both feeling, they slowly gathered their belongings and packed the car. The drive back to Virginia's house was a quiet one. Sam walked Julia to the front door. The young couple had already said their emotional goodbyes throughout the morning. Neither had any desire to make a spectacle for all the neighbors that watched from their windows. They hugged for a long time and, as he stepped back, Sam kissed her gently and quickly. Her lips were slightly swollen from the intense passion of their earlier affection but they were very soft. Julia stood on the porch as Sam walked back to his car. Knowing he would not want to linger after saying goodbye to Julia, Sam had taken care of his goodbyes to his grandparents the evening before. Julia began crying again as Sam backed out of the driveway and drove slowly down the street. Although they made the normal promises of keeping in touch, Julia was sure they would not do so. They would for a time but, eventually, life would get in the way and the letters and phone calls would become fewer, with longer periods of time between. She entered the house and found Virginia sitting at the kitchen table with a freshly-made cocktail which she pushed across the table toward her. Julia sat down heavily and the quiet crying grew more intense. Virginia got up and walked behind the young girl and wrapped her arms around Julia's shoulders.

"Hurts like hell right now, but it will ease a little at a time," she said to her niece.

"That's.... what.... I'm.... afraid of," Julia managed through the choking sobs.


When the hurricane cleanup was finished at the end of the summer, she took a part-time job at a small family-owned grocery store in town. She missed Sam much more than she ever imagined was possible. They spoke on the phone two to three times a week and wrote long, loving letters. When autumn drew near, Julia began to feel restless. Her high school friend Anna had recently moved to Phoenix and Julia started to think about moving there. For several weeks, she debated the pros and cons of moving so far away. She would be closer to Sam.

# Handsome Stranger

Marie and Julia fell comfortably into a routine. Marie usually took her cup of coffee to the garden and sat quietly as the birds began their morning songs. Occasionally, Julia would join her and it was during these times Marie was able to coax more stories from her. Although Julia always feigned a resistance to talk about herself, Marie saw the twinkle in the old woman's eyes and it was obvious she relished the chance to tell someone of some of her life stories. The pair ate a light breakfast; afterward they went downstairs to the store.

As the weeks went by, Julia showed Marie more and more about the operation of the small business. Had she taken the time to think about her reasons for giving Marie added responsibilities, Julia would have realized she was grooming the girl to someday take over the store. Her psyche did not allow her think that she would someday not be able to run it herself. Having been a stubborn, independent woman, it had been difficult for Julia to accept the help of others. She had such a deep need to be self-sufficient and self-reliant that it was nearly impossible for her to step back and allow others to help. Though she had only known Marie for a short time, Julia saw much of herself in the girl; it was sometimes eerie.

Marie got to know the people of the small town that shopped at Julia's store and she generally recognized everyone she saw. One afternoon, she returned from the storage room with a box of canned goods to restock the shelves. She heard the ring of the bell when someone entered. She walked toward the front of the store and ran head-first into a tall, broad-shouldered man who appeared to be near her age. She looked up into one of the most handsome faces she had ever seen. His eyes were a piercing blue and Marie swore those eyes outshone the largest diamond.

"Ouch!" he said, loudly, but with a wide grin.

Only then did she notice she had dropped the box on the stranger's foot.

"I am so sorry. I hope I didn't really hurt you," she said nervously as she bent down and picked up the scattered cans.

She reached for a can of corn that rolled toward his opposite foot and saw he wore study work boots.

"You didn't even feel it, did you?" she said when she stood and met his gaze.

"Of course, I did. I think you might have broken my toe," he replied as seriously as he could manage.

He reached down to help pick up the remaining items from the floor and carefully placed them into the box. He picked up the refilled box and hoisted it onto his shoulder. Marie had not realized she was staring, and she turned her head quickly to hide the blush that spread across her face. Without asking where she wanted the box, he turned and walked around to the next aisle and began placing the cans on the shelf. Something about the way he moved confidently through the store piqued Marie's interest. She had never seen him before, but she could tell he felt comfortable and had been there many times. Just as she opened her mouth to ask who he was, Julia came through the back door.

"When did you get here?" Julia asked with a touch of excitement Marie had not heard before.

"About five minutes before this woman assaulted me with vegetables," he answered through a low chuckle.

He walked to Julia, threw his arms around her, and picked her up. He squeezed her into a hug that Marie thought would crush the old lady.

"How you doin', JuJu?" he asked as he put her down gently.

"Old and cranky, what'd'ya think?" she said, attempting to sound like a crotchety old hag.

"JuJu?" Marie asked.

"Yep. My grandmother here may pretend to be a sourpuss but she's sweeter than any jujube honey ever made in Morocco," he answered with a sideways smile to Julia.

"Don't let him fool you, Marie. His nickname for me is nothing quite that exotic. He calls me JuJu because he couldn't say my name until he was damn near five years old."

Although she truly did try to appear to a be a life-hardened, cynical, old woman, Marie saw the love and pride Julia felt for her grandson. It was that love that came through in the woman's voice and her body language.

"So, you're Marie. I've heard a lot about you from my mom. The way she talked about some stranger coming in and taking over JuJu's store, I thought for sure you'd look like a troll and shoot flames from your eyes if anyone got too close."

Horrified and speechless, Marie stood there with her mouth open. Her eyes glistened with tears that soon spilled over.

"Oh no, no, no, don't cry. I am so sorry. I was just joking; she's only said good things about you. I didn't mean to hurt your feelings," he said quickly.
He extended his hand and introduced himself. "My name is Jason and I'm really not the jerk I just appeared to be."

Still stunned, Marie took his hand, gave a firm handshake and tried to act as though his words had not affected her as deeply as they had.

"Are you two quite finished making asses of yourselves while you just leave me standing here?" Julia asked as she looked from Marie to Jason and back to Marie again.

"How do you think he grew so damn big?" she asked Marie.

Before the girl had a chance to think of a response, Julia answered her own question. "From all the feet he's put in his mouth over the years!"

She laughed and turned to walk to the front of the store. "Get it? He's big. He's many *feet* tall," she said over her shoulder.

Thinking Julia was out of hearing range, Jason turned to look at Marie and whispered, "She's got a very weird sense of humor."

"I heard that! I may be older than dirt, but I still hear just fine young man!" Julia yelled from the counter.

Jason looked at Marie with exaggeratedly wide eyes and she laughed loudly. He walked toward the counter and Marie stared at his firm butt in the perfectly fitting jeans. Julia looked up as the two walked around the corner and caught the slight smile cross Marie's face.

That evening the trio sat at Julia's tiny dinette table and ate a meal of roast beef sandwiches, potato salad and homemade barbeque potato chips.

"I'd like to apologize again for making you cry earlier," Jason said to Marie.

"No, don't worry. I embarrassed myself when I bumped into you and dropped the box on your foot. When you said what you did, I was just caught off guard and overreacted," she answered somewhat shyly.

"So, JuJu, I'm sure you've been telling Marie some of your stories," he said.

He turned to Marie and asked, "Where'd she leave off?"

"Going to Phoenix," Marie answered.

# The Adventure Begins

For the second time that year, Julia packed everything she owned into her car. She and Virginia said their goodbyes and Julia began her long journey; stopping first at her parents' home to spend a few days with them before she headed west.

As he had done before she left home for South Carolina, her father checked her car to make sure everything was in working order. Julia knew he was trying to delay her departure as long as possible. This became clear when she saw him check the same belts and hoses for the fifth or sixth time.

"Daddy, I'll be fine. The only way you could possibly inspect anything closer would be to take the whole thing apart," she said as she leaned over to look for herself.

He turned to face her and she read his thoughts.

"Don't you even *think* about it, old man!" she said, grinning. "I've got to get going in the morning. Anna is waiting on me. I promise, everything will be ok."


Having arrived safely in Phoenix, Julia began the process of staring her new life. She got a job, found a small apartment and began meeting new friends. She helped Anna with her growing family. She took long runs through the various trails in the area. For months, her life was laid-back and easy. Thanksgiving and Christmas were tough since she was so far away from her family, but she managed to fill the time and enjoy the holidays by doting on Anna's small children. Throughout this time, she and Sam continued to speak frequently and he planned a trip to Arizona in the early spring. With something exciting and new to look forward to, Julia's days began to pass quickly.

The day before Sam was due to arrive, Julia began to get nervous. Theirs had been such an intense romance when they were in South Carolina. Julia worried things would not be the same when she saw him again.

Her fears were dispelled when Sam arrived. A single look told each of them that the love they felt for one another was not simply a steamy, summer romance.

They spent their days touring the city, going to museums, walking through the many parks. The evenings were a mix of plays, night clubs and fine dining. Nights were spent with such passion and urgency, they collapsed exhausted into a deep slumber, wrapped in each other's arms.

As expected, their time together was coming to an end too soon. Just as it was when Sam left South Carolina, the morning of his departure was emotional. He delayed leaving as long as he could. They made their promises to write and call; the difference this time being that each knew the other would follow through.

Julia returned to her normal routine. She occasionally went out with friends, but most of her days were spent working, then returning home to an empty apartment. She and Sam talked frequently but the phone calls were not enough. Although neither would say it out loud, they both began to realize it was increasingly harder to have a relationship without being in the same place.

One evening, Julia sat on her back porch and watched the moon's assent into the clear sky. Lost in thought, it took her a moment to realize someone was ringing the doorbell. Thinking it was one of her neighbors, she was taken by surprise when she opened the door to find Sam standing there.

"Sam! What are you doing here?" she asked with an excitement she could not contain.

"I can't' do this anymore," he said.

Julia's eyes filled with tears and she turned quickly to walk back into the apartment. Sam followed her and soon realized she thought he meant he cannot continue their relationship. He walked up behind her and wrapped his arms around her waist. He felt her stiffen.

Hugging her close, he leaned down and whispered, "I just can't be away from you."

She turned around to face him quickly and threw her arms around his neck, burying her head into his chest.

"I thought you meant..."

"I know. I'm sorry. I shouldn't have just blurted it out like that."

Julia went to the kitchen to pour them each a glass of wine; and to allow herself time to regain her composure. She returned to the living room, handed Sam his glass and sat down beside him on the couch.

"So, what is it that you're proposing?" she asked.

"Well," he began, then took a large sip of wine. "I guess I'm, um, proposing," he said as he placed his glass on the table.

Leaning slightly to the side, he reached into his pocket and pulled out a small box. He turned to face Julia and cleared his throat. He reached out and took her hand and placed the box in her palm.

With shyness Julia did not think possible from this man, Sam asked, "Will you come to Wyoming and marry me?"

Everything seemed to be happening so fast. It had been a mere two weeks since Sam proposed. Lost among her thoughts, Julia did not realize she was still standing in front of the half-packed box. Small strands of fine hair that had come loose from her ponytail floated around her face. The print from the newspaper she used for wrapping had turned her hands black and she saw smudged fingerprints along the side of the glass she held. From the moment he handed her the small jewelry box, Julia never hesitated or questioned her decision to say yes. Even though the decision was made quickly, she had no doubt she made the right move. Marrying Sam and moving to Wyoming was exciting and she felt she had never been as happy as she was in that moment. It was difficult to turn in her resignation at work and even more so to tell Anna she was leaving.

In just a few days she would be on her way to Wyoming and her new life with Sam. Excitement, anxiety, hopefulness and a little trepidation were the whirlwind of emotions that flooded through her. Julia reminded herself that feelings of apprehension were normal when such a huge change was made. Above all of her underlying thoughts and emotions was the happiness. She continued each day to pack up her life in Phoenix and soared on the high she felt. Sam would be returning in a few days and their new life would begin.

The last box was loaded onto the truck. With pent-up, nervous energy, Julia paced the empty living room as she waited for the apartment manager to come collect the keys. Even though the apartment was completely empty, and she had checked several times, Julia opened cabinets and drawers and closets and conducted yet another search to make sure she did not leave anything behind. She opened the coat closet in the hallway and heard Sam snicker.

"What?" she asked.

"You've checked that closet at least five times in the last half hour. We got everything, stop worrying," he replied.

"Oh, shut up," she said with a grin and a giggle.

The landlord arrived, and she and Julia walked through the apartment checking off the items on the move-out list. Julia checked again to make sure her forwarding address was on the paperwork and handed over the keys.

As Sam and Julia drove away, she asked him if he double checked the back patio. He replied that he had, each of the ten times she asked him to do so. He turned on the radio and tuned into a classic rock station, knowing that music was the best way to calm the restless beast next to him. Their plan was to drive to Arches National Park in Moab, stopping there to eat and rest.


The glow of the setting sun intensified the rich colors and defined the many cracks, crevasses and cave-like erosions of the rock. The clouds in the sky that were white and puffy moments before changed to a myriad of pink tones. The varying shades seemed to both highlight and contrast the rich copper colors of the surrounding rocks. The formations in the distance appeared so small compared to the open spaces that seemed to go on forever. Julia looked toward the horizon and saw the never-ending world beyond. So many of the holes and arches created over time were so perfectly placed, it was difficult to imagine they were caused by nature rather than being man-made sculptures. It was quite overwhelming to comprehend the extreme length of time it took for each shape to be created on the ever-evolving landscape.

"It's just so beautiful," Julia whispered. She felt she was gazing upon hallowed ground and speaking in normal conversation tone seemed irreverent.

"Yes, it is," Sam replied, matching her low volume.

They knew they needed to get back on the road, but it seemed blasphemous to leave before the sun was fully set. The skies turned slowly to vibrant orange then melted further into red until, at last, the sun sunk below the edge of the horizon and the skies darkened. They reached the car and turned in unison toward the west, caught sight of the tiniest speck of light and watched in awe as it went out.

His head rested against the window, Sam snored softly next to her as she drove east toward Denver. She turned the radio down low and allowed the warm, happy feelings to flood over her as she drove. She was still anxious about the move, but the stress of that morning was long forgotten and relaxation took over.

# There's No Such Thing As A Fairy Tale

Julia awakened from a deep sleep. For what seemed an eternity, she lay there and tried to remember where she was, or even when it was. Slowly it all came crashing back to her.

*As she does most mornings, Julia sits on the front porch of the small house drinking her coffee and watching the sun rise. It is a beautiful morning and there is a crispness in the air. The sun gilds the heavens as it creeps upward; beginning as the color of butter but becoming more vibrant as it peaks over the horizon. Slowly the clouds glean the roseate highlights, changing to fuchsia as the morning begins. Directly east, she can just make out the salmon-orange star as it emerges. The fiery disc first sparks, then explodes into a bonfire; its flames igniting the clouds as they sweep westward. She is hypnotized by the deepening colors and soon the clouds are bathed in a multitude of oranges and reds. This cinematic display ends and, too soon, the firmament loses the flaring shades and begins to mimic a field of daffodils. Julia sits back in the huge chair on the porch and is soon lost in the latest book she has been reading.*

*She has been reading for several hours when she is slowly pulled from the book's imaginary world and realizes she can hear horse's hooves in the distance. Putting the book down, she gets up and walks down the steps to the yard and looks out over the open land. Sam and the other ranch hands left before dawn and were not expected back until late into the evening. Julia stares ahead and can just begin to make out the shapes of men riding on horses. The group draws closer and Julia recognizes the horses and the men. She hesitantly takes a few steps toward the oncoming entourage and simultaneously notices that people have walked out of the big house and have begun to also walk toward the group. A strong sense of dread falls over her and she stops in her tracks. It is in this moment that Julia notices the travois being pulled behind one of the horses. Everything is happening in slow motion and Julia recognizes the horse as Sam's. She tries to convince herself that he is only injured, but the expressions on the faces of those walking toward her tells her it is much worse. Unable to hold her own weight any longer, Julia drops to her knees. Dismounting his horse and coming to sit beside Julia, the head rancher gently places his arm around her shoulders. Through her sobs and the ringing in her ears, Julia is just barely able to make out what the man is saying.*

*"His horse got spooked by something and reared up,"* the gentleman begins. *"Sam was thrown from the saddle and broke his neck when he fell."*

*Several of the women help Julia get to her feet and walk her slowly toward the house. Just before reaching the porch, Julia breaks free and runs to the side of the house where she bends over and vomits.*

Soon after Sam's death, Julia decided she could not stay in Wyoming. The wounds were too fresh and everything about her surroundings was too painful. Having made arrangements to return to Phoenix to stay once again with Anna and her family, Julia began the heartbreaking task of packing her things. Although she felt she could not take it all, she decided to take a few of Sam's treasured items and made sure to take some of her favorite items of his. She soon found herself lost in thought and had no idea how long she had been sitting on the bed hugging Sam's coat breathing in his lingering scent. Suddenly, she jumped up and ran to the bathroom. Afterward, she rinsed her mouth and returned to the bedroom to finish the task at hand.

Hours later, the car was packed and she began to say goodbye to the friends from the ranch. She hugged Lillian last and, as she made the promises to keep in touch, she felt a sudden urge and ran to the side of the house.

"Maybe you should wait a day or two, you seem to be coming down with something," Lillian said when Julia returned.

"Thank you, Lil, but it's just all of the emotions –," Julia replied. "I think I just need to get away. I'll be fine."

The long drive from Cheyenne to Phoenix proved to be more daunting than Julia expected. She turned on the radio in hopes of distracting her thoughts but the music prompted memories instead of drowning them out. She switched from recalling a happy moment, even managing to smile, to the water-works flooding to the point of having to pull over. She realized it was the music that caused the bounce between happy and sad and tried to drive for a time in silence. However, that proved to be worse so she cranked the volume up and decided to just go with whatever came.

# Someone New

Julia allowed herself a few weeks to heal and to decompress after her return to Phoenix. During this time Anna noticed that Julia seemed to be getting thinner. She heard Julia in the bathroom several times and hoped her friend had not become bulimic.

"You've been eating properly, right?" Anna asked one evening.

"Yes *mom*. I just sometimes have trouble keeping things down. Don't worry so much. I'm sure it's just all the stress. It'll go away—," Julia replied trying to put her friend's mind at ease.

Julia forced herself to move forward. She contacted her old employer and was thankful to be able to return to work there. She was soon able to find an apartment and began the process of starting her life over. The weeks went by and, although she felt she was in a dream, she managed to establish a routine. One evening after work Julia stopped by the grocery store to stock up on a few items. She mindlessly roamed up and down the aisles, not paying attention to the items she has picked up. She glanced down to see what she still needed and noticed she had placed some feminine products into the cart. Although she did not remember taking them from the shelf, seeing them in the cart made her think back to the last time she purchased any. She left the cart in the aisle and walked in a trance-like state toward the register with only the single item in her hand. She returned to her car and, without any forethought, drove to Anna's house. Not expecting her friend to stop by that night, Anna gave Julia a confused and questioning look. Without making eye contact, Julia handed a small bag to Anna and walked into the house.

As she passed through the foyer, she said in an unusually flat voice, "I need to pee".

Rather than walking toward the bathroom, she instead dropped into the recliner in the living room. Confused by her friend's odd behavior, Anna opened the bag and peeked inside. What she found was a small box.

Looking at Julia she asked, "When was it you started having trouble keeping your food down?"

"When Sam..." Julia began but stopped short. She looked momentarily confused. "No. Wait. It was right before. We

thought I'd eaten something bad. After that, I just assumed it was because of everything that happened."

"Sweetie," Anna began, "that was months ago."

"Uh huh," Julia responded vacantly.

Anna pulled the box out of the bag and reached for Julia's hand.

"I guess you'd better get in there and do some peeing then," and handed the box to Julia.

Once Julia was finished in the bathroom, the two women sat in silence awaiting the result. When the tiny pink plus sign appeared, a single tear fell down Julia's cheek. She was overcome with both grief and joy and started to cry uncontrollably. Anna could only sit and hold her, helpless to do anything else to comfort her friend.

"That must have been wonderful and horrible at the same time" Marie said.

"Oh, honey, you have no idea. One moment I was on top of the world, the next I was in the depths of hell. As if there weren't enough reasons to be emotional, I had hormones raging to boot," Julia replied.

"How in the world did you get through it?"

"I just did. It wasn't like I had any other choice. You do what you must do to get through one day, then another, and another. You just keep going because there isn't any alternative."

"So, what did you do after you found out?"

Several months later, Julia made the decision to return home to Atlanta. Although Anna had been a tremendous help during the months following Sam's death, Julia felt she needed to be near her family. A friend of Anna's, whom Julia had met on several occasions, had been looking for a place, and Julia made arrangements to sublet the apartment to her. Again, Julia packed everything she owned and drove across the country.

She took her time driving and stopped often to rest. During the day, she rode with the radio up loud while she sang along. Julia had begun to feel the baby move days before leaving Phoenix. She was driving along singing loudly to a rock song with an exceptionally heavy beat when the baby became extremely active. Each movement was in time to the music -- Julia imagined her unborn child dancing.

Julia awakened just before dawn. She remained in bed trying, unsuccessfully, to ignore the need to go to the bathroom. She worked late into the night and had only been asleep for a few hours. It soon became evident that she was not going to be able to hold off any longer. Her belly was huge and she was not able to sit up, so she inched toward the edge of the bed and rolled off. Exhausted, she nearly fell asleep as she sat on the toilet. She was aroused by the slight cramping of her stomach. It was quite mild and went away quickly. She finished in the bathroom and returned to bed hoping to get a few more hours sleep. After what felt like only moments, she was awakened by the urge to go to the bathroom again and saw that it had been almost two hours since she was up last. Again, she rolled herself off of the bed and walked to the bathroom. Just as she sat down, her gut cramped again.

"I knew it was a mistake to eat those chili fries," she said aloud.

She knew she would not be able to go back to sleep so she turned on the radio and laid on the bed to relax. Soon though, she got up and made her way to the bathroom for the third time. Curious, she grabbed a small windup clock from the dresser and took it with her to the bathroom. She noted the time of the cramp. Ten minutes later, another one hit. Continuing to sit in the bathroom, she watched the minutes tick by. When the next wave came exactly ten minutes later, she mentally backtracked and tried to calculate the time between each of the cramps this morning. Within five minutes, her belly tightened again. There was no more question; she knew she was in labor.

Julia retrieved her bag from the closet then called her mother.

"Hi, Mom."

"Hi, sweetie. What are you doing up already? Didn't you work last night?" her mother asked.

"I did. The baby didn't give me any choice. It's time Mom."

"Time for wha... Oh my gosh! Really? Do you need us to come pick you up?"

"There isn't enough time. The contractions are already five minutes apart. I'm leaving now."

In the delivery room, the nurses got Julia ready for the birth. The head nurse checked the progress and told Julia she was dilated to a two. Before the nurse's aide could get a sheet draped over Julia's legs, the door opened and a hospital staff member attempted to lead a strange man into the room.

Startled at the sight, Julia sat up and yelled, "That's not the father!"

For a moment, everyone in the room froze and the confused man in the doorway had a look of shock on his face. Quickly, the man was escorted back into the hallway. Julia collapsed back onto the pillows and a small tear trickled down her cheek.

Moments later, the first strong contraction hit. When it was over, the nurse helped Julia find a comfortable position. Over the next thirty minutes, the contractions became more intense and closer together.

"When is the doctor going to get here?" Julia asked one of the older nurses.

"He'll be here before too long," the woman replied in a nonchalant manner.

"He'd better get here soon, it's time for me to push."

"Honey, I've been doing this a long time and I always know when it's time to bring in the doctor. This is your first baby, you're gonna be here for quite a while. You just need to lie back and try to relax."

Seething, Julia said through gritted teeth, "Listen here, you condescending bitch, this may be my first time giving birth but I'm telling you, whether I push or not, this baby is on the way."

Deciding to pacify the hysterical patient, the nurse patted Julia on the hand and, with lips pursed, said, "We'll take a look-see and find out how dilated you are now. Then I'll let you know when the doctor needs to be here."

Knowing that the nurse was only checking the progress to prove a point, Julie felt quite vindicated when the woman's eyes opened wide and she began barking orders.

"Get that damn doctor right now," she said to one of the other nurses. "Tell him the patient is fully dilated and I can see the baby."

One of the nurses handed the pink bundle to Julia. Looking down into the still-red face, Julia whispered, "Hello Emma. I'm your mama," and gently kissed the baby on her wrinkly forehead.

Julia unwrapped the baby from the blanket and softly caressed her fingers and toes and stroked the head of black hair. She noticed the baby's long nails.

"Will you clip her nails, please?" Julia asked the nurse.

"We can do it later. She's fine for now."

Quietly, but with command, Julia said, "I'd rather it be done now" while she pointed to her own cheek. "That's how I got this scar. I scratched myself the day I was born."

Having witnessed the fury Julia displayed when she was contradicted earlier, the nurse wisely chose to fulfill the request.

Try as she might, Julia could not fall asleep. Though her body was exhausted from the delivery earlier in the day, her mind would not rest. She got out of the bed and walked quietly to the nursery to see Emma. Standing at the window looking down at her daughter, Julia began to cry. Though silent at the start, the tears began to flow more heavily and her sobs became more prominent.

Thinking the new mother was just suffering from exhaustion and the baby-blues, a nurse walked out to the hallway and asked Julia if she was okay. Julia nodded but the emotion consumed her and soon she was crying uncontrollably. The nurse guided Julia to a chair in the nurses' station and handed her a box of tissues.

"It's okay, sweetie. A lot of new moms feel this way. It's just your hormones running wild."

Speaking between the sobs, Julia said,
"You...don't...under...stand. It...it...it's not...that."

After several minutes, Julia was able to pull herself together enough to tell the nurse about Sam. When her story was finished, the nurse leaned over and gave Julia a small hug and patted her on the shoulder.

"You wait here," the nurse said quietly. "I think I know just what you need."

She went into the nursery, then returned to the station with Emma in her arms. She gently handed the baby over to Julia, who was again overcome with emotion.

A few minutes later the nurse asked, "You wanna keep her in your room with you tonight?"
Julia was only able to nod. The nurse stood and took the tiny baby from the young mother's arms and said, "You go back to your room now. I'll bring her down in just a bit."

She sat on the porch watching and listening to the rain. The cool breeze flowed across her bare arms and caressed her face. It was in moments like these she let her mind wander. For many people, the clouds and rain recalled sad memories. She loved the rain. She loved the sound and the smell and the way it washed away the dirt and grime. For her, the rain evoked happy memories. An opening in the clouds allowed the sun to peak through. In the distance, the vibrant blue of the sky and the white purity of the puffy clouds were sharp contrast to the gray directly overhead. The green of the grass and the orange, red and yellow of the autumn leaves intensified as they were cleansed by the rain. Soon the rain lessened, the clouds began to clear and the world sparkled as the sun reflected off the water droplets.

Through the open bedroom window, she heard Emma as she began to coo. She took one last look at the glistening backyard and went inside. She opened the bedroom door and smiled at her precious daughter with the sleepy grin and crazy, fuzzy hair.

One afternoon Julia was cleaning the kitchen while Emma played quietly in her room. It was a pleasant day and Julia had the front door open to allow the gentle breeze to come through the screen door. The little girl had recently begun to walk and Julia kept a keen ear on the child's wandering about the tiny apartment. Julia walked to the hallway to get a clean dishtowel from the linen closet. As she was returning to the kitchen she peaked into Emma's room. It was empty. Julia called out to Emma but there was no response and she was quickly aware of the absolute silence. Just as she entered the living room, she noticed the screen door was slightly open. Frantic now, she ran to the door and looked outside. Emma was toddling across the small yard toward the street. Julia knew if she yelled, or ran after her child, Emma would think it was a game of chase and would run in the direction of the busy road. Slowly, Julia opened the screen door and stepped onto the porch. Walking toward the little girl, Julia had to remind herself to not run. She closed in on the child and could not resist any longer. In two large steps, she managed to close the gap and scooped up her daughter just as she lifted a foot to take the final step off of the curb. Adrenaline was rushing through Julia. Hugging the baby tight, she turned toward the apartment just as a car sped by. The enormity of the event came crashing down and Julia began to cry. Confused, Emma reached over and wiped away her mother's tears and kissed her on the nose.

Julia and Emma were visiting her family in Atlanta. As the family gathered in small groups chatting, Julia's uncle was talking with Emma. Jon was telling a tall-tale. Emma listened intently as her beloved Unca-Jon rambled along with his nonsensical story. He included outlandishly wrong information and misdirection but Emma never interrupted. His bizarre story finally came to an end and Emma looked sweetly into his eyes. She knew he was trying to fool her and, with a sly grin creeping across her sweet face, said "Is that not right."


Emma had been exceptionally clingy throughout the day. Julia was playing a board game with some of the other adults and Emma wanted to show her something.

"Mommy, come look."

"I will in just a minute baby. We're almost finished with the game and then I'll go see."

"No, Mommy, now!"

"Emma, you can wait just a little while. I promise I will look just as soon as the game is over."

The little girl stomped off in a huff and mumbled something Julia could not distinguish.

"Hey baby girl, knock it off. I'll be there in a few minutes."

The game soon wrapped up and Julia went to see what it was that Emma wanted to show her. She looked in the bedroom but Emma was not there. She searched for her daughter throughout the house but could not find her.

"Has anyone seen Emma?" she asked the others.

Julia walked outside and looked around calling out Emma's name but there was no response.
"Seriously? None of you have seen her?" she asked again. No one had. Together they all began searching through and around the house but the girl was not anywhere to be found. Julia started to panic.

"I'm going to drive around the block," Julia told the group.

She drove around the circle and then down the dirt road that ran behind the house to the trailer park but she still did not see her daughter. She drove around the block again quickly filling with dread. As she approached the house, she could see several people standing on the front lawn. There, in the middle of everyone, stood her daughter.

Julia barely had the car to a full stop before she slammed it in to park and leapt out. She ran to her daughter and fell to her knees while grabbing the confused child into her arms in a tight hug.

"Mommy, you're squishing me."

"Sorry, baby" Julia said through the tears.

"Why are you crying mama?"

"I'm just so happy to see that you're safe. Where were you?"

"I fell asleep under the bed."

Julia looked up at the others, "At least three of us looked under the bed."

"No, three of us looked under from one side" her father replied. "The leaves for the dining table are stacked under there. It wasn't until we looked from the other side of the bed that we could see her. She was curled up sound asleep."

"I'm sorry, mama. I got mad at you and hid under the bed."

"Mom, can you come get me?"

"I thought you were spending the night."

"I was but I don't feel so good."

"Okay. I'll be there in a few minutes."

"I'm not at Mandy's."

"What do you mean? Where are you?"

"I'm at the skate park."

"What? Never mind, we'll talk about it later. I'm on my way."

As soon as Julia pulled up to the park, she could tell something was not right. Emma looked awful. Julia was worried about what may have happened but, as soon as the girl started walking toward the car, it was obvious. Emma opened the car door and Julia was hit with the distinctive odor of alcohol.

Emma closed the door and Julia began to drive. Each of them was silent for the trip home.

Julia pulled into the parking space and Emma began to say something then quickly opened the door and leaned out. The sound was bad enough, but the smell was worse.

"At least you didn't do it in my car!"

"Mom, please, can we talk abou..."

Emma threw up again and groaned as she made her way toward the apartment.

"What the hell did you drink?"

"Vodka."

"Emma, you're only thirteen!"

"Mom, I'm begging you, can we just talk about this later?"

# Some Things No Child Should Know

"You sick bastard! What the hell makes you think that is even the least bit funny?" Julia heard Marie scream at the man in the store.

"Whoa! Chill out bitch and get the fuck out of my face!" the man yelled back.

"Hey, what the bloody hell is going on here?" Julia asked Marie.

"This scumbag needs to leave now before I…" Marie began.

"Before you what?" Julia interjected.

"Before I… I don't know!" Marie turned and ran through the store and disappeared to the back.

"My apology, sir," Julia said to the man standing there dumbfounded.

"That's one psycho you've got there lady," he muttered.

"What happened?"

"Beats the hell out of me. I was just talking to my buddy and the next thing I know that girl got in my face and started screaming at me."

The man and his friend left the store and Marie was quite sullen for the remainder of the day. Later that evening, Julia and Marie retired to the garden as was their routine.

"You gonna tell me what that was all about today?" Julia asked.

"I'm so sorry, Julia. There was a young girl in the store and that dirt bag made a crude joke about her to his friend. I couldn't believe I was hearing such vulgar language talking about a child."

"Okay, but that still doesn't explain why you went off on him the way you did."

"I guess it's just years of anger built up to the boiling point."

Marie took in a long, deep breath and began to tell Julia of her darkest secret.

Although she had been told there were no monsters in the closet or under the bed, the summer of her parents' divorce Marie discovered that monsters do exist. They disguised themselves as normal, upstanding citizens. They led the world to believe they were doting single fathers who made incredible sacrifices to raise their children alone. They paraded around and pretended to be a part of the human race and they knew exactly who to target and how to draw them in. After that summer and fall, Marie knew her life had been forever altered and that average-appearing people sometimes wore masks to hide the hideous truth.

Marie watched as the new tenants moved into the complex. She was interested more than her friends because, until a few months earlier, her family lived in the unit the man and his daughter moved into. Marie was eager to introduce herself to the little girl, who was close to her same age. As Marie approached the girl, a woman walked out of the apartment to retrieve a box from the car. Marie assumed the woman was the little girl's mother, but she would later learn she was in fact a nanny that sometimes stayed with the girl and her father. Focused on making her acquaintance with the little girl, whose name was Chelsey, Marie did not notice the odd way the father looked at her, or the strange look the nanny gave to the man.

For the better part of the next week, Marie and Chelsey spent quite a bit of their playtime together. Even though they sometimes played outside, or at Marie's home, they usually spent their time at Chelsey's. They played games, or watched TV, or sat in Chelsey's room listening to records. One day, Chelsey's father was sitting in the living room playing his guitar. He was not very good, but Marie enjoyed listening. At the time, he was learning to play Johnny Cash's "Wayfaring Stranger." Seeing Marie's interest in the instrument, the man handed the guitar to her and asked if she wanted to learn to play. She said she did and he started showing her the finger placement for some simple chords. Standing behind her, the man reached around and held her hands to show her how to hold the guitar properly and how to adjust the pressure her fingers placed on the strings. Completely unknown to Marie, the man had just made his first move in what was an evil plan. As the next couple of weeks went by, the man drew her in deeper and deeper into his sadistic web; first by showing her the guitar, then by showing her how to use a soldering kit. So enraptured was she in what he showed her, Marie did not realize how much of the time she was alone with the man. When the man began inviting her to spend the night with Chelsey, Marie's mother thought nothing odd of it. The girls had been spending so

his hand cupped around the end of his penis, he went into the bathroom. Unsure what she was supposed to do, Marie stayed where she was. The man came back into the bedroom and asked Marie to get up onto the bed. She started to pull up her shorts and panties but he told her no and said she should take off all of her clothes. Marie did what she was told and looked up at him as he approached the bed. He reached forward and gently grabbed her ankles and slid her to the edge of the bed. He got down on his knees and began kissing her legs. With each kiss, he moved further and further up her legs. Soon he was kissing her on her vagina. He slowly spread her legs apart and then lowered his face to kiss her again. This time, Marie felt something hot and wet push through the slit and move up and down on the bump between. At one point, he stopped and asked Marie how it felt. She replied that it tickled. He chuckled slightly and began once again to use his tongue to stroke her. He increased the pressure and moved his tongue faster. Moments later, Marie was confused and scared by the convulsive movements her body was making. She tried to stop it but did not have any control over the shaking of her abdomen and legs. Unsure what was happening, she told the man it tickled too much. It was not until years later that Marie would learn that what happened to her body was an orgasm and that it was the same thing that happened to him when he made those noises and made a wet spot.

For how long the abuse went on Marie had difficulty remembering. When she thought about it in later years, the best guess was that it happened over a period of a few months. She only remembered that it happened after her parents separated in the spring and that it was still happening at Halloween; but it must have stopped soon after that because she did not remember it being cold outside.

"You know, I've never spoken to a single soul about that summer," Marie said hoarsely.

"My God child! What a horrible thing to live through," Julia answered. Beyond that she was speechless.

"The one thing I can be thankful of is that he never actually... you know..." *"Really Marie? You can tell her about everything in such detail and you can't say the word penetrate?"* she thought.

"Did you ever tell him no when he asked you to do something?" Julia asked.

"Once. He showed me a picture of a little girl, she was probably about eight or nine, on her knees in front of a naked man. Of course, the man was only seen from the waist down. She was holding his penis with both of her tiny hands and had it in her mouth. He asked me if I would do that to him. The girl looked like she was gagging and all I could think was 'she's gonna throw up.' I thought it looked really gross. I told him I didn't want to but he just said maybe someday we'd try that."

Marie fell silent for a time and Julia could tell she was trying hard to get the image of the helpless girl out of her mind.

Marie took a deep breath and continued. "He took pictures of me sometimes. He would tell me how to pose, sometimes he had me masturbate. I've often wondered if I ever appeared in any of those magazines and, if I did, was it any of the pictures that showed my face."

Wiping tears away, she said, "I've never felt guilty about what happened to me. I never felt like it was my fault or that I was the one that did anything wrong," she began. "But there are two things I have always beat myself up over."

"What's that?" Julia inquired.

"Because I never told anyone, he probably assaulted other girls, possibly even his own daughter. I might have been able to stop him, but I kept quiet – just like he told me to."

"That would be a lot to cope with, but I don't think you should blame yourself. You were just a little girl and couldn't have known that you had any power to do anything. You said there were two things," Julia replied.

Marie took another deep breath and, with tears re-forming in the corners of her eyes, continued. "There was a part of me that enjoyed it."

Several minutes went by before Julia had the courage to ask Marie what she meant.

Gathering her composure, Marie went on. "Not the mental or emotional part of me. But, on a physical level, some of what he did was pleasurable to my body and my body reacted. I had orgasms."

"No! No! No! You listen to me missy, and you listen good. 'Pleasurable' is not what that was! Anatomy and biology and chemical reaction is what that was. There are many things our bodies do that have nothing to do with pleasure, or any other emotion. Sometimes it just reacts. Sometimes there is nothing more to it than how a raindrop bursts when it hits the ground. Just because your body reacted back then the same way it does when you are with someone now, does not mean it was pleasurable or that you liked it. It only means that your body exploded with endorphins and caused a kind of euphoria that let your mind erase the horrible things that were happening to you."

With a tiny smile beneath the tears, Marie leaned over and hugged the old woman. They sat for a very long time; Julia consoling that lost little girl who had carried such a tremendous burden for so long.

"He called me once, a few years later. The idiot said we couldn't see each other anymore because he had to go away for a while. I think he said he was in Shreveport but I don't remember for sure," Marie said quietly.

"What did you do?"

"You know, that was actually one of my proudest moments. I told him I hoped he burned in Hell and that he better not ever contact me again and that if he did, I was going to tell the whole world what he did. All I kept thinking after I slammed down that phone was that 'going away' meant he'd finally been caught. I've hoped and prayed over and over that was what happened and that he got payback in prison. Did you ever notice that even the most hardened people, guilty of unspeakable crimes against other humans, have no tolerance or mercy for people that hurt kids, especially if it's sexual abuse?"

Raising the wine glass in her hand, Julia proclaimed, "To all of the thieves, murderers, and deranged, here's to you for doing to the molesters what they've done to poor children everywhere. May all of the vile thieves of innocence and murderers of childhood be tortured beyond imagination and rot in Hell for all of eternity!"

"You're crazy, old woman," Marie said while shaking her head and rolling her eyes.

"I do have a couple of questions though," Julia said. "You said there was a nanny that was there sometimes. Didn't she ever notice something weird or make any effort to stop him?

"Oh, the nanny was a different story. You see, you'd have to be a sane person to realize something like that was happening in the next room. That woman was completely looney. She swore she was a witch and would cast spells on all of us. I didn't know what it was called back then, but I know now that the one word that truly describes her is 'psychotic'. If she knew, she never said or did a thing. In fact, I wouldn't be surprised if she was actually helping him. I was too young to know about such a thing, but sometimes I think he or the nanny were drugging Chelsey. She just fell asleep too easily and stayed asleep for too long."

"And your parents or teachers? Didn't they notice you acting differently or sense that something was wrong?"

"They all saw a change in my personality but, remember, this was happening at the same time my parents were going through a divorce. Everyone around me naturally thought it was the breakup of our family that caused me to change. Like I said, he knew exactly who to target, who was the most vulnerable and pliable."

# The Rabbit

One story at a time, Marie began to open up more and more to the older woman. For the first time in her life she feels as though she can talk about anything and not be judged. Although Julia often gave advice, sometimes more than Marie wished, she never once made Marie feel inferior or belittled her in any way. Marie did not realize until years later but having someone with whom she could confide her deepest secrets and fears helped her face her demons and lock them away. She would forever remember what Julia once told her. *'We all have our demons. Some we can fight and destroy, but some we have to capture and chain up in our dungeons. The most difficult part is to remember that the ones we've placed in prison are still there, that we ensure the restraints are good and tight and that we should never give the key to someone else to hold. Only then can we remain free to have the life we are meant to live.'*

*Deciding it would be best just to get it over with, she blurts out "I'm pregnant." When she remembers this conversation months later, she realizes the look he tried but could not hide, should have been a clue as to how this would turn out.*

*The two young people just sit in silence as the enormity of their situation sinks in. Marie had already made up her mind to keep the baby but she was unsure what Tom's reaction would be. With every intention of following through, Tom promises to be there with her and to marry her. The first few weeks go by and it looks as though they will be a happy little family. They find a small apartment and Marie gets a job in a tiny neighborhood bar. Unfortunately, what begins as a fairy tale soon begins to turn into a horror story. Marie begins to notice changes in Tom's personality and appearance. He leaves each morning to go to work but when he comes home, he stinks of alcohol and goes straight to bed. It is not until Marie asks Tom to pick up some groceries one day that the reality she has been blind to starts to crash down on her. Tom says he does not have any money and finally admits that he was fired from his job and has been going to a friend's house every day. Reminding him that they have a baby on the way, Marie begs Tom to find another job, which he promises to do.*

*One day, while Tom is out looking for work, there is a knock at the door. It is the landlord. He informs Marie that he is evicting them and says she and Tom have to be out of the apartment by the end of the week. When Tom arrives home late that night, he*

again smells of beer and Marie tells him they have to move. Against rational judgment, Marie once again allows Tom to convince her everything will be okay. Several days later, they pack up the few belongings they have and move into a pay-by-the-week hotel. Their room is a tiny efficiency apartment with a kitchenette. Although it is furnished, the pieces are old and the bed has been used by more people than Marie cares to think about. As Marie is brushing her teeth that night a large, black roach crawls out of the drain. She tells Tom she is going to take a hot shower. She is soon thankful for the alone time and the sound of the water because she just stands under the stream and cries. Drying off and regaining her composure, she goes into the room and sees Tom sprawled out across the bed sound asleep. She manages to tuck herself into the small corner of the bed and, only because of the emotional exhaustion, finally falls into a troubled sleep.

The small amount of money Marie is making at the bar is just barely enough to buy a few items at the store. Although she gets bread, milk, eggs and some peanut butter whenever she can, there is rarely much to eat. On the days Marie works at the bar, she eats until she feels she will pop. However, on the days she is home, her stomach is usually growling. Marie finally realizes just how desperate the situation is when she and Tom walk to the Dairy Queen up the street and use the change they have managed to find and buy a single hot dog to share. As Tom breaks it in two and hands her the slightly larger portion, Marie happens to notice the woman sitting at the table watching them. Embarrassed, Marie quickly walks away and Tom must jog to catch up to her.

Over the next few weeks Marie does her best to pretend her life is not the catastrophe it has become. One day, while at work, she begins having cramps in her stomach. Assuming it is hunger, she does not let anyone know and attempts to keep quiet. The pain intensifies and she finally tells her boss she thinks something is wrong. Noticing that Marie is very pale and seeing reflected on the girl's face the amount of pain she is in; the bar owner tells Marie she needs to go to the emergency room and offers to give her a ride. With no way to contact Tom, Marie accepts the ride and asks one of the regular customers at the bar to let him know what happened if he came by.

When the doctor says the horrible word "miscarriage," Marie tries not to hear it. She immediately begins blaming herself. The hospital staff is used to seeing women distraught over this news,

but one of the nurses suspects there is something else going on with Marie. She sees that the girl appears to be malnourished and asks the social worker to stop by. During her conversation with the counselor, Marie admits she has not been taking care of herself and has not been eating. The social worker recommends Marie be kept overnight. She tells Marie it is just for observation, but she is hoping to get the girl to eat a healthy meal. The next morning, while being discharged from the hospital, Marie is given a card with the name and address of a local food bank. She has not seen or heard from Tom, so Marie calls the bar and asks the owner to come get her from the hospital. Reluctantly, Marie tells her boss about the food bank and the two of them stop by so Marie can get a box of food. Returning to the hotel, Marie expects to see Tom there but the apartment is empty. Scared and confused, Marie just sits looking out the window watching for him to return. Late that night, Tom stumbles in. He is drunk and Marie quickly realizes he has been doing drugs of some kind. She tries to tell him about the miscarriage but his drug and alcohol daze is too deep. He mumbles something and drops into the bed. Several hours later, Marie hears Tom get out of the bed and go outside. Assuming he has just stepped out to smoke a cigarette, she rolls over and goes back to sleep.

The early morning sun is shining through the window and a ray of sunlight pierces through the thin drapes and Marie awakes. Tom is not in the bed. She gets up to use the bathroom and afterward goes into the kitchenette for some water. She sees her hospital discharge paperwork scattered on the table and knows Tom has read them and knows about losing the baby. Thinking he has gone out for a walk to clear his head, Marie decides she will make them a nice breakfast with the food she received from the charity. Opening the refrigerator, she sees that quite a bit of the food is missing. It is not until then that she looks over toward the little closet and sees that some of Tom's clothes appear also to be missing. Stunned, she drops into one of the kitchen chairs and just stares at the table.

Naively hoping that Tom will come back, Marie returns to work the next day and busies herself as much as possible when she is at home. After a week, she must admit to herself that Tom has abandoned her. Without any friends in the area and too proud to admit to her family she has made a horrible mistake, Marie decides she should get away from here and start over somewhere new. She packs all her clothes into her shabby suitcase and makes as many peanut butter and jelly sandwiches

*as she can with the bread that she has left. Using the last of the money she has earned over the past week, she buys a bus ticket. She has no destination in mind but she has enough money to get to Payson, Arizona.*

# Discovering Love For The Second Time

"Tell me about Hank," Marie said to Julia one evening as they finished dinner.

A warm smile crept across the wrinkled face.

"Ah, my sweet Hank. There isn't a day that goes by that I don't miss him. After losing Sam and raising Emma by myself, I never thought I'd find anyone else, much less actually settle down. I won't say he was my best friend, that's too cliché, but he *was* my friend, my confidant, my equal and my biggest supporter. I never doubted his love for me and he never doubted mine for him. Falling in love with him was easy. Emma wasn't too keen on the idea at first, but she came around."

"Why didn't she like him?"

"She never disliked him necessarily, but it took some time for her to accept him. She'd had me to herself her entire life and that was the first time she had to share me with anyone. She was fifteen when I met him and she behaved like a typical self-centered teenager. Once, early on in my relationship with Hank, Emma got mad at me because she wanted to me take her somewhere but I'd already made plans with him that night and I told her no. She had the nerve to say I cared more about him than her."

Marie's eyes opened wide. "What did you do?"

"I told her to shut the hell up, that she didn't know what she was talking about, and that she knew damn well that wasn't true. I told her she may be the *most important* person to me, but she wasn't the *only* person in my life. It was a bit tense for those first couple of years, but she eventually settled down and allowed herself to get to know him. Naturally, once she did that, she grew to love him as much as I did. He never tried to be her father, just her friend and in the long run she saw what a wonderful person he was and was proud to call herself his daughter."

"So, how did you meet him?"

"At work."

She arrived at the office one cold January morning to find her supervisor speaking with a man she did not recognize. As she stowed her belongings in the desk drawer, the two people approached. The man was introduced and Julia shook his hand. With broad shoulders and large hands, the man's name, Hank, seemed to be fitting. She sensed a bit of sadness in his blue eyes and a certain devilishness in his grin, both of which let her know she would enjoy working with, and getting to know, this man. Within the first few weeks of meeting, Hank and Julia began to develop a friendship of teasing, laughing and a comfortableness with each other. It was not long before the rumors began to make the rounds at the office. The water-cooler talk only increased when Hank, having learned that Julia lived a short distance from him, asked if he could ride with her for the next few days while his truck was in the shop. Seeing Hank and Julia arrive and leave together each day, their co-workers assumed they were romantically involved. Although the two continually denied any involvement with each other, it became harder and harder to convince everyone when Julia's car broke down and she and Hank began again to carpool. It was not until a night out with several of their fellow employees, when Hank flirted and danced with a young girl at the bar, that the rumors were finally silenced.

For months, the friendship grew. Even though Julia's car had been repaired, the two continued to carpool often and shared with each other stories of their past or talked of current events. Julia was with Hank when he learned his teenaged niece was pregnant. She was with him when he received the call from his mother letting him know the family dog died. They talked about music and old lovers. They swapped tales of their teenage antics. Julia vented her frustrations over trying to raise a teenage daughter alone. They became so comfortable around each other that soon no topic was too embarrassing or too private to discuss.

On a Saturday in late June, Hank called Julia to ask her about some items she ordered that would be needed early Monday morning. Telling him it would be easier for her to look for the information rather than try to explain over the phone where to locate it, Julia volunteered to meet him at the office. She arrived twenty minutes later and was able to quickly confirm that the items would arrive in time. Since they were both hungry and had no other plans for the day, the two decided to get some lunch and pal around for the afternoon. They went to a bar in their neighborhood where they ate, drank a few beers, played pool, and watched some baseball games. Julia told Hank of the time she was nearly fired from her job as a cocktail waitress.

As she did occasionally after clocking out, Julia remained at the bar to have drinks with friends. She usually had only a few before going home, that night however she decided to stay. The bartender was a heavy pourer and the cocktails were strong. Soon Julia was quite relaxed and more than a little inebriated. The band's lead guitarist came down from the stage, moved through the crowd and climbed atop the main bar to play his solo as he did each night. Feeling no inhibition, Julia decided she wanted to dance. She crawled onto the barstool then to the bar and stood beside the musician. When the solo started, Julia began dancing without a care in the world. She was thoroughly enjoying herself until she looked down to see the bar manager as he stood below her. Julia could not help but giggle when she saw the look on his face. He was obviously not amused and, without a word, pointed to her then to the floor. She sat on the edge of the bar and the manager offered his hand to help her down. He said nothing at that moment, but when Julia arrived for work the next day, he read her the riot act.

"If you ever do anything like that again, I'll fire you on the spot" he said sternly.

"I really am sorry. I was just trying to have fun" she replied.

"Fun is one thing but do you realize what a liability I'd have on my hands if any of the customers decided to follow your lead?"

Neither one had plans for the evening and decided to find somewhere to have drinks and sing karaoke. Since she had only brushed her teeth and thrown her hair into a ponytail when Hank called earlier in the day, Julia said she really needed to get cleaned up first and said she could pick him up when she was done. They arranged a time to meet later that evening and each went home.

Over the years Julia tried unsuccessfully to pinpoint the exact moment everything changed that day. Whatever, or whenever it happened, something inside her clicked that summer day. Julia would be forever thankful that she acted on those feelings. She did much more than simply shower that afternoon. She carefully applied her makeup and styled her hair. She chose a pair of jeans Hank had once complimented. She arrived to Hank's house at the planned time. As he got into the car he said, 'Well, somebody got all dolled up,' to which Julia casually replied, 'Just felt like looking like a girl tonight.' They had barely reached the end of the

block when Hank, now feeling quite underdressed, asked her to go back so he could change clothes.

In the years to come, Hank would admit that the single thought that went through his mind when Julia picked him up that night was 'Oh, shit! This is a date!' After months of denying they were anything more than friends, and finally convincing their coworkers that nothing more was happening, it was ironic that the two began that day as friends but ended that night as lovers.

"Sounds like it wasn't just the people you worked with you were trying to convince," Marie said.

"My mother told me I was resisting. I guess I was. I'd been on my own for so long, I wasn't sure even how to be in a relationship anymore. Hell, I dated a little bit while Emma was growing up, but nothing was ever serious or lasted more than a few dates. I certainly had no expectations of any of those men being around for any length of time. And, I suppose I was protective of Emma too. She never knew her father so I didn't want to bring just anyone into her life."

"Tell me more about him," Marie requested.

The two women sat in the garden for hours while Julia told one story after another about her years with Hank.

They drove north on Highway 87 out of the city; thousands of saguaros standing at attention as Julia and Hank left the concrete jungle and headed to the mountainous wilderness of the Mogollon Rim. Soon the cacti were replaced by towering pine trees and the road began to wind its ascent far above the valley below. The arid desert transformed into a lush forest. Six thousand feet above the Phoenix elevation, an entirely different world waited. Gone was the traffic, the pollution and the heat. As the road snaked its way higher and higher, Julia could feel the stress and anxiety of everyday life melt away.

They decided to have a picnic at Woods Canyon Lake. The two sat quietly on a rock that overlooked the small lake and watched the families below in their paddle boats, the little boy whose father was teaching him to fish, the ground squirrels chase each other, and the eagles that soared overhead. Julia closed her eyes, took a deep breath and exhaled slowly. At 7,500 feet above sea level, the air was so completely pure it made her slightly dizzy.

"This is *exactly* what I needed today. Thank you, babe," Julia said.

Hank smile, put his arm around her shoulders and kissed her cheek. "Me too babe, me too."

"The sun is going to start going down soon. Should we head over to the Rim?" Julia asked.

They gathered their belongings and made sure not to leave any trash behind. They drove with the windows down and savored the cool breeze that blew across their faces. Following the dirt road, they found a small area with no one around. They walked to the Rim and found a large rock with a perfect view of the mountain range and the descending sun. The forest below was a combination of dark shadows and sunlit swathes of varying shades of green. Two thousand feet below, the tiny headlights of a single car could be seen winding along the two-lane road that led up the escarpment.

"This never gets old," Julia whispered.

Julia sat on the rock and took in all of the sights, sounds and smells. This was her church. The tall pines the congregation, the wind through the trees and the chirping of the birds were her choir. It was in this place she was able to clear her mind. This was where her sanity returned and she felt thoroughly relaxed. As

the sun began to set, the colors of the forest were intensified. The browns of the rocks became brilliant orange, the clouds above glowed with deep yellows, rich oranges and fiery reds. Only the highest peaks of the mountains could be seen on the horizon when the sun exploded with its finale then moments later was gone.

"The grandeur of nature is too spectacular for words," Julia said. "We become the voyeur and she the exhibitionist."


He was gone again. It did not happen often, but Hank sometimes became restless and needed to get away. He drove sometimes for hours, listening to music and enjoying the solitude. Early in their relationship, Julia wondered why Hank felt he could not share his thoughts and feelings when he sank into this melancholy. It worried her to know that there were some things that affected him so deeply yet he kept them to himself. As the years passed however, she grew to understand that he did not discuss it because there was not anything specific to talk about. It was during these times that even Hank himself could not put into words what he was feeling. It was vague and impossible to pinpoint, and the only way to get through it was to get behind the wheel and disappear for a little while. When he returned, he conveyed in some manner or another how much he loved her and how happy he was to be with her. For this she was grateful; he always returned and he always let her know she was an important part of his life.

Hank arrived home to find Julia standing half-naked in front of the open freezer. He knew how much she hated the summer heat, but that year was worse. That year, not only was she suffering from the intense desert temperatures, menopause was settling in and she was having hot flashes. She closed the freezer door and Hank laughed when he saw her flush face with sweat running down her nose.

"Shut up," she said playfully.

He reached up, wiped off the drop of perspiration, and kissed her on the tip of the nose.

"I can't do this anymore," she huffed. With those words uttered, she was suddenly thrust back in time.

*"I can't' do this anymore," he says.*

*Julia's eyes fill with tears and she turns quickly to walk back into the apartment. Sam follows her and soon realizes she thinks he means he cannot continue their relationship. He walks up behind her and wraps his arms around her waist. He feels her stiffen.*

*Hugging her close, he leans down and whispers, "I just can't be away from you."*

*She turns around to face him quickly and throws her arms around his neck, burying her head into his chest.*

*"I thought you meant..."*

*"I know. I'm sorry. I shouldn't have just blurted it out like that."*

*Julia goes to the kitchen to pour them each a glass of wine; and to allow herself time to regain her composure. She returns to the living room, hands Sam his glass and sits down beside him on the couch.*

*"So, what is it that you're proposing?" she asks.*

*"Well," he begins, then takes a large sip of wine. "I guess I'm, um, proposing," he says as he places his glass on the table.*

*Leaning slightly to the side, he reaches into his pocket and pulls out a small box. He turns to face Julia and clears his throat. He reaches out and takes her hand and places the box in her palm.*

*With shyness Julia did not think possible from this man, Sam asks, "Will you come to Wyoming and marry me?"*

"Babe!" Hank said loudly and shook her gently.

"Sorry. Flashback," she replied.

"You can't do what anymore?" he asked.

"The heat. I just can't stand the heat. I don't think I can make it another summer here."

Over the next few months they discussed the possibility of moving away. They talked of going to Show Low or leaving the State entirely to go somewhere like Oregon or to the Carolinas. As the weather cooled, they spoke of it less but Hank always remembered how desperate Julia seemed that day in the kitchen.

One evening in the early fall, Hank asked, "What do you think about moving away from Phoenix?"

"I've been thinking of either the woods or the beach," Julia answered without hesitation.

"Payson has woods."

"So, Payson it is then!" she said definitively.

# Forests And Beer

Julia sat alone in the garden. She could hear Marie through the open kitchen window. She knew the young woman would come out to join her soon. She adored the girl and was thankful for the company, but she also reveled in her time alone. She tilted her face upward to meet the warm morning sun and thought back to her last day in Phoenix.

*She sits alone in the small backyard holding a steaming mug of aromatic coffee. The first blush is her favorite time of day. Above her, the half-moon glows. On a clear day, she can see the faint shape of the entire moon but today it is cloudy and the night orb is enveloped in a cottony corona. Wrapped tightly in her robe, she watches the sky as it changes. Morphing from blue to white, the sky looks as though it is being bleached by the coming sun. A herringbone band of gun-metal gray clouds stretches endlessly across the sky, the strip breaking apart as it glides across the ocean-like veil. The sky begins to lighten and soon the billows imitate white caps rolling toward the shore. The first rays of light pierce through the trees casting long shadows across the yard. The aviary melodies begin as the birds awaken and join as one chorus, giving sound to the morning canvas. A single bird takes flight and one by one others joint him. Julia watches as the flock soars and glides through the air, their silken winds dappled by the now risen sun.*

*Watching the sunrise is a daily ritual for Julia. Today though she diligently absorbs the scene so that she may never forget the incredible beauty. Today is the last time she will see nature's glorious display above this desert landscape. Today, she and Hank will begin a new chapter in their lives.*

*"You about ready?" Hanks asks, causing Julia to jump, spilling some of her coffee.*

*"You scared the hell out of me!" she barks.*

*Unable to refrain from laughing, Hank says, "I'm sorry babe. I thought you heard me coming."*

*"Sneakin' up on me, makin' me slosh my coffee everywhere," she grumbles.*

*Leaning down, Hank gently kisses her neck and whispers, "You're going deaf old woman."*

*Jumping up and turning toward him, she squawks "Who the hell you callin' old?"*

*"Who me? I didn't say anything. Got no idea what you're talking about," he begins. He reaches out and wraps his arms around her waist, pulling her toward him.*

*"Um hmm. If you think huggin' on me is gonna make me forgive you, you've got another think comin'," she replies, trying hard to be mad at him.*

*"Oh, you'll forgive me," he says quietly as he brushes her hair away and again kisses her neck. "How about a quickie before we go?"*

*"Such a romantic," she says. A sheepish giggle escapes as she grabs his hand and leads the way into the house.*

*Julia later grunts as she gets up from the floor. "I'm too old for this," she mutters.*

*"Thought you said you weren't old," Hank teases.*

*"Oh, shut up. I'm still mad at you."*

*"Tell yourself that all you want, but I know you're not."*

*"What makes you think I'm pretending?"*

*"Your accent gets thicker when you're tri-yun to be angry."*

*Julia sticks her tongue out, then walks toward the bedroom to get dressed. As she proceeds down the hall, Hanks says, "I see your butt." She gives a little wiggle and they both laugh.*

Too soon Marie came out to the garden and sat down across from Julia. Marie sat silently, absorbing all the sights and sounds of the wakening day.

"I was thinking about my Hank," Julia said quietly.

"How did you know for sure he was the one?" Marie asked.

"He made me laugh, but it was more than that.  You know that soft and warm feeling you get when you first have a crush on someone new?"

"Ya."

"Well, that feeling never left.  Every single time that man walked into a room, he made my heart smile.  It didn't matter if he'd been gone for five minutes, five hours or five days; when I looked at him, I felt that same tingle in my gut.  Don't get me wrong, he could surely piss me off, but no matter how angry I got, deep inside I still got butterflies."

They sat quietly for several minutes, then Julia continued.

"You know, it's funny, Hank never thought of himself as the romantic type, but he really was.  I think, to him, it wasn't romantic unless it was moonlight, candles and soft music.  He did so many little things that were so thoughtful.  Whether it was something simple or something that took a lot of planning, he always seemed to know just the right thing to make me happy."

"Like what?" Marie asked.

"One year for my birthday, he got a small hutch and made it into a coffee bar.  He filled it with various coffees, flavoring syrups and bought an espresso machine.  Every morning, when I opened the cabinet, it was like walking into a coffee shop.  It gave me a little heaven to start my day."

"Lord knows you love your coffee," Marie interjected.

"Just be glad you've never had to be around when I didn't have my morning coffee!  There was also the astronomy Christmas."

"The what?"

"Hank knew how much I enjoyed the sky.  Whether it was watching a sunrise or a sunset, or gazing at the moon and stars, or just pointing out shapes in the clouds.  For Christmas one year, he surprised me with a trip to Kitt Observatory in Tucson.  The evening started with a small interactive class about the moon.  We did an exercise where we all stood in a circle around a lamp with the shade removed.  We each had a pencil with a Styrofoam ball attached.  We held the pencil out in front of us and slowly turned around.  As we turned, the lighting on

the ball changed signifying the different phases of the moon. They also had an activity that showed how, due to the lack of atmosphere, the moon's craters never change unless something else hits the moon. They had pans filled with flour and we dropped different size pebbles into the pan and created craters. Each time we dropped another rock near an existing crater, it would create a new one or would change the shape of the previous one. While they were setting up a small telescope outside, we all watched the most incredible sunset. Once the moon began to rise, we took turns viewing it through the telescope. The big finale was going into one of the observatories and having the opportunity to look through one of the more powerful telescopes. The trip to the observatory happened a couple of weeks before Christmas. My present on Christmas day was a small beginner's telescope."

Grinning, Julia said, "One of the best things about our time together is that we laughed often. Sometimes it was over something silly that no one but us would find humorous. Did I ever tell you the story of the cat attack?"

"Your big yellow cat you had when you were little?" Marie replied.

Chuckling, Julia said, "No. The cat Hank and I had when we were in Phoenix. We had only been together for a few years when we took in a stray kitten. She was really sweet, but she would go haywire every now and then for seemingly no reason. Well, one night, she either got a wild hair up her ass, or decided it was time to play and she pounced with claws out onto Hank's leg."

"What he'd do?"

"Well, he yelled of course, but we started laughing so hard we couldn't finish," Julia said with a grin.

"Finish what?" Marie asked naively.

Giggling, Julia said, "Let's just say we were quite occupied at the time."

The two women laughed until tears were pouring down their faces.

Finally, able to speak through the hysterics, Marie said, "Thanks a lot for the visual old lady! I'll never be able to look you in the eye again."

"That man made me laugh right up until the end. I don't remember what he said or did, but I remember us giggling even as he was dying."

Julia fell silent for quite some time and, when Marie looked over, she could see that Julia's eyes were closed. The light from the moon illuminated a single tear running down the old woman's cheek. Moving quietly so not to disturb Julia, Marie got up and went back into the house to allow the woman to have some private time.

Julia knows she will not have him much longer. When he was first diagnosed, she wanted him to fight, she researched all the current treatment statistics and began gathering information for all of the best facilities. Hank did not want any of it. He did not wish to go through the horrors of radiation or chemotherapy. She begged him to reconsider but he would not budge. He told her that he did not want his final days to be wasted and said that treatment would only keep the inevitable at bay for a short time. She was angry for the first few months but, when it became evident she would not be able to change his mind, she was forced to accept the fact that their time together would be ending soon. He managed to hold on for nearly a year but recently the pain became too much to bear and the doctors put him on a morphine pump. He slept most of the time but this morning he seemed to be more lucid. Throughout the day, they talked and laughed and Julia began to fool herself that perhaps he was improving. Sitting in the hospital room this evening, however, she had to concede that he would likely not make it through the night. Lost in her thoughts, she did not initially realize he was awake.

"Hey babe," he said quietly.

Smiling through her tears, she leaned over and kissed his cheek. "Hey you."

She looked into his eyes and read what neither of them wanted to say aloud. Pulling back the cover, Julia slipped into the bed beside him. Though he was weak, he was able to hug her tightly. She gripped him as hard as she dared and they held each other in silence for several minutes.

Some time later, Julia felt his arm relax a bit. She lifted herself up onto one elbow and looked up at him.

"I love you more than you will ever know," she said through her tears.

Moments later, she felt the rise and fall of his chest stop.

As she leaves the hospital that night, a nurse approaches Julia and gives her an envelope with her name in Hank's handwriting on the front. Once she arrives home, she opens the envelope to find a CD with a note that read "For Julia." She inserts the CD into the computer. Across the screen scroll the words "Our love story." Set to the Pearl Jam songs "The End" and "Just Breathe"

*is a video collage of pictures of Julia's and Hank's years together. Sitting in the house she now occupies alone, Julia cries and replays the video several more times.*

Looking to the now-empty bedroom, Julia leans against the door frame. She is smiling and crying as the memories flood over her. She had never been one to have an emotional attachment to a home, but this time was different. This was the last house she and Hank shared. Over the years she had begun to associate every nick in the wall, every chip in the tile, every stain in the carpet with her memories of the time the two spent together building a home. She knew it was an impossible reality but her imagination roamed and she could smell his scent and hear his breathing.

"I miss you so much," she says to the vacant space.

She walks over to the far wall and slowly runs her hand over a spot where the sheetrock is damaged. A small giggle escapes as she remembers how the dent was created. She had been on a ladder cleaning the ceiling fan. As she stepped down, the ladder tilted and fell against the wall. Hearing the loud bang, Hank came running into the room thinking Julia had fallen.

"Holy shit woman! You scared me to death--!"

"Relax babe, I'm fine. I just knocked it over," she replied as she walked over and placed a hand on his chest. Resting her head on his shoulder she said, "You worry about me too much."

Hank wrapped his arms around her shoulders and hugged her as though he could never let her go.

Slowly, Julia returned to the present and saw she had a light blanket draped over her lap and shoulders. Julia looked toward the other chair and saw Marie sipping a cup of tea. On the table between the two was a teapot, another cup and a small plate of lemon wedges.

Julia smiled at the thoughtfulness of the young woman.

"Welcome back," Marie said, breaking the silence of the night.

Day after day, the two continued their routine. Coffee and a light breakfast in the garden to watch the sunrise, then work and a simple dinner after they locked up the store. They spent some evenings together but usually spent time quietly by themselves.

One afternoon, as the two restocked the shelves, a man entered the store and stood staring at the large stained-glass window.

Julia walked over to Marie and whispered, "Here we go again," and approached the man.

"Can I help you?" she asked.

"Hi ma'am. I was wondering if you have ever considered selling this window."

"Not even once--," Julia responded curtly.

The man was visibly taken aback by the gruff tone. "Oh. Okay then," he managed to say.

"Sorry mister. I didn't mean to be... well, mean. I've just been asked the same question hundreds of times over the years. That, and I'm a cranky ol' bitty--," she said with a wry smile. "But to answer your question in a more dignified manner, I appreciate the interest but I designed this window and it's very special to me. I really have no desire to part with it."

Smiling down to Julia, the man extended his hand and said, "Fair enough."

Once he was gone, Marie walked over to the window and asked, "You really designed this?"

"Sort of. Remember I told you about the bar where I worked, the one I almost got canned from for dancing on the bar?"

"Yes."

"Well, they had a similar window. When Hank and William and I opened the bar, the first thing I did was start having this one made."

"So, this store *was* a bar. I've wondered."

Marie saw the faraway look on Julia's face and knew another story was coming.

"It was so much fun. A lot of hard work and long hours, but it was mostly fun. Opening that bar was the best thing that ever happened for my Hank. Until then, he just never felt he'd accomplished anything worthwhile."

"From the things you've told me, it sounds like he was quite successful," Marie interjected.

"He was, but it took him a very long time to *feel* like he was. When we first moved to Payson, we had a furniture refurbishing business. Hank would find old pieces and restore them into beautiful works of art. It was a thriving business and many of the pieces he created are still around town. There is an old desk in the lobby of City Hall and a magnificent floor-to-ceiling bookcase in the children's section of the library. The counter in the store used to be the main bar. It was in extremely poor condition when we first bought the bar, but Hank worked his magic and turned it into something wonderful. The original piece was much bigger. When I converted this place into a store, it was too big so I had a section of it removed. The part that was taken out is in the bookstore next door."

"Did he make your bed too?" Marie inquired.

"He did, sort of. It's actually parts of several different pieces of furniture that he reconfigured into the frame and headboard. It has to be broken down into about ten pieces whenever it's moved, otherwise no one would ever be able to lift it."

"I wondered how you managed to get it up there."

"I really thought the furniture business would be the catalyst to get Hank out of his feelings of failure, but it didn't. You have to understand that, one some level, I was responsible for him not feeling worthy," Julia said.

"That's hard to believe. The way you talk about him, it sounds like you were always his best supporter," Marie replied.

"Well, I always felt a bit guilty for it anyway. You see, when I was young, I was going to take over the corporate world. I didn't go to college, but I was going to bulldoze my way through the good ol' boys

club and prove I was better than all of them. Of course, I hadn't expected to be a single mother who just needed to make ends meet. If I had pursued my dreams then, I wouldn't have been able to be the mother to Emma that I wanted to be. A few times through the years I thought about taking some classes and getting back to that dream, but something always seemed to get in the way. As I got older, that dream slowly waned and by the time I met Hank, all I really wanted to do was retire early. Once we moved here, my strongest desire was to stay at home sewing, writing, doing arts and crafts, cooking and learning to can fruits and veggies. Hank knew this and he wanted to be able to give that to me more than anything else. When he couldn't, he felt like he failed. In so many ways he was like my grandfather. Granddad was 'just an Iowa farm-boy' as he liked to say. He survived being a POW in Germany, came home from war and went to school on the GI bill and met a sweet and funny Texas girl and raised his children to be good and kind and thoughtful. With all of that, he still felt like he was not successful because he couldn't make it as a traditional businessman. No one could ever convince him that his determination, strength and willingness to try something new were all exceptional qualities his children and grandchildren would admire and strive to duplicate. I tried my best to encourage Hank, but you just can't *make* someone see something they *can't* see. Anyway, after we opened the bar, Hank finally found his niche. I think, for the first time in his life, he was content. He felt useful and successful and he learned to be at peace and allow himself to be truly happy.

# Hank & Willie's

An unsettling yet sweet, decaying aroma permeated the stale air inside. Standing in the dim light, Julia asked, "You're sure about this?"

Hank and William looked at each other then, in unison, replied "Absolutely!"

"Don't you two think we're all a bit old to be taking on such a monstrous endeavor?"

William casually replied, "Hey, if we fail, we fail. Let's live a little and take a gamble."

Julia walked silently through the building to inspect the walls and floors. It was obvious the bar had been empty for quite some time and had been neglected long before it closed.

Leaning toward William, Hank said, "We got 'er. She's already remodeling in her head."

"I can hear you, dork. You never did learn how to whisper," Julia called back over her shoulder.

Her survey completed, Julia walked over to the two men. Placing her hands on her hips, she looked at the pair and saw a gleam in their eyes. "My God, you two look like little boys on Christmas morning." She drew in a deep breath and exhaled slowly. "The first one that tries to drink away the profit gets kicked out on his ass. Understood?"

"Yes'm," William answered as Hank leaned in and picked Julia up in a crushing bear hug.

In the months that followed, the three spent their days gutting the inside of the dilapidated bar. When the demolition was over, the only remining item was the long, winding oak bar. Although it required refinishing and reinforcing, the massive piece was still in surprisingly good condition. Hank and William, with help from a few of the young men in the neighborhood, replaced the flooring, the walls, and the cabinetry and built a small stage. Meanwhile, Julia spent her days perusing antique stores and second-hand shops to look for decorative items. Much sooner than any of them expected, the remodeling was completed and they were ready to open for business. The night before their grand opening, the three friends made a final walk-through.

"Entrée, mademoiselle," Hank said as he held open the door for Julia.

"Merci, monsieur," Julia responded as she exaggeratedly waltzed through the doorway.

Julia and Hank stood in the dark while William fumbled to find the light switch. In that moment, Julia turned to her right and looked up to the saloon girl illuminated by the glow of the street lights outside. Once the lights were on, Julia stood and surveyed the finished product of their hard work.

To the left of the door stood an old juke box that had been reconfigured to play Internet-based music instead of forty-fives. A narrow shelf-like bar ran the length of the left wall. Sturdy wooden bar stools were lined up just under the bar. The front wall above the juke box, as well as the left wall above the smaller bar, were covered in pictures of the Old West. Julia procured many old sepia photos from various museums, galleries and antique shops. These framed photos were peppered between posters and promotional pictures from 'Ponderosa', 'Wyatt Earp', "Gunsmoke' and numerous other Wild West television shows and movies. One photo of the 'Gunsmoke' cast was Julia's favorite. To anyone that looked at the photo detail, it was obvious that Miss Kitty was the inspiration for the stained-glass saloon girl. Between the front door and the dance floor stood fifteen tables, each with four chairs. The 20'x20' dance floor was once in a ballroom dancing school and the years of use made the surface perfect for gliding along in a two-step. Above the dance floor was a small stage. It was not anything elaborate and was just big enough for a drum set, a keyboard and two to three people out front. A small stairwell led from the back of the stage to a narrow hallway to the office and stockroom. To the left of the stage, a

larger set of stairs led to the sports bar upstairs. The main bar extended along the right wall. The previously dilapidated oak bar had been expertly refinished by Hank and was velvety smooth with a high sheen. Keeping the inventory simple, the bar was stocked with six beer taps and basic hard liquors. Hanging on the wall behind the bar was a massive painting of wild horses running across a beautiful green valley between two large, snow-capped mountains.

The downstairs bar was Julia's territory. Upstairs, however, was the work of Hank and William. Three of the four walls displayed a multitude of televisions. On the wall opposite the bar, one large television was flanked by two smaller ones. A dozen stainless steel topped tables took up much of the space between the entrance and the bar. The bar top was covered in distressed stainless steel. Thick-cushioned bar stools lined the "L" shaped bar. Along each of the walls, between the televisions, hung pictures and posters of football, baseball, basketball and NASCAR. Football and baseball jerseys and memorabilia were mounted to the walls, scattered among the pictures and TVs. The wall behind the bar had a large Plexiglas case that contained some of the more valuable or sentimental pieces of sports memorabilia. Glowing throughout the space was neon in many colors.

"I never did ask you boys what was up with that big-ass pickle jar," Julia said as the three walked through the upstairs area.

Hank walked behind the bar and pulled out a shaker with six dice inside. He reached into his pocket and pulled out a dollar bill which he dropped into the jar. He then poured the dice onto the bar as he explained. "One dollar gets you a roll of the dice. Anyone that gets a Yahtzee gets half of whatever money is in the jar. The other half we'll donate to one of the local little league teams."

"Looks like you didn't get squat. Here, let me try," Julia said.

"Where's your dollar?" William asked.

"Put it on my tab!" Julia teased.

The bar was packed that night. Hank and William had been tending bar upstairs but had both come down. Generally, at least one of them remained upstairs to supervise but Julia did not think it odd for them both to have left their usual stations. It seemed that a larger number of the regulars appeared to be lingering downstairs. Julia assumed that they stayed to hear the new band play. As William walked around and talked to the patrons and to the band members on break, Hank came behind the bar to help Julia. When he saw the band return to the stage, Hank asked Maggie to keep an eye on things and asked Julia to help him restock. Walking toward the supply room, Hank suddenly took Julia's hand and gently led her to the dance floor as the band began to play Eric Clapton's "Wonderful Tonight."

"I thought you said you needed help," Julia said with a sheepish grin.

"Who me? What makes you think I can't get a few bottles of booze all by myself?" he replied coyly.

They danced slowly and Julia rested her head on Hank's chest. They rocked side to side and Julia could feel the reverberations as Hank sang along with the band. It was not until the song was over and everyone began to clap that Julia noticed that she and Hank were the only people dancing. She took an exaggerated bow. She reached up and gave Hank a kiss on his cheek and started to turn away but Hank would not let go of her hand. Facing him, she began to ask what he was doing when she noticed he had something in his other hand. Very slowly, he knelt down and, while doing so, slipped the ring on her finger. For a moment she was frozen. They had joked for years that they would never get married and here he was proposing. Realizing he was waiting for an answer, Julia quickly nodded her head. The entire bar erupted in applause, whistles and shouts.

"Have you ever thought about getting that chip in the window fixed?" Marie asked.

"I did have it fixed. You should have seen what it looked like before. Did I tell you about the night it was broken?"

Marie shook her head and Julia told her.

> One night a drunk customer told Julia she should turn the bar into a XXX movie house and call it "Yank Your Willie" instead of "Hank and Willie's." Julia told him to shut up but he continued. He became more and more belligerent and tried to climb over the bar. Hank and William escorted the man out and he tripped going through the door and bumped his head on the sidewalk. Angry, the man picked up a rock and threw it at the stained-glass window. Furious, Julia ran outside, picked up the rock and threw it at the man, hitting him square in the lower back.

"Oh my God! You actually threw a rock at a customer?" Marie asked.

"Sure did! The idiot actually tried to sue us for injury but the case was thrown out. You know, I never knew for sure if he really tripped on the way out the door, or if Hank and William helped him."

"How did you always manage to make good decisions?" Marie asked Julia one evening.

"Trust me honey, I haven't *always* made the best choices. Haven't I told you about the time Emma and I had to move in with Hank and his brother?"

"Huh, uh."

"Hank and I had only been seeing each other for a few months. I had changed jobs about a year before so I had a period of time when I didn't bring home a paycheck, I made arrangements to pay the rent for my apartment on the fifteenth of the month instead of the first. I thought the woman I made that arrangement with was the manager but it turns out she was just one of the office staff. She had been processing my rent checks on the fifteenth of each month without the knowledge of the woman that really was the manager. When the manager found out, she sent me a letter letting me know I would have to start paying on the first of the month beginning that October. I got

to the letter at the end of August so I went ahead and paid my September rent on the fifteenth as I had been doing. One day, near the end of September, I arrived home from work to find an eviction notice on my door and the locks changed."

"What the hell?" Marie exclaimed.

"Yep. I marched down to the leasing office to see what the hell was going on. It turns out, right after sending me that letter, the manager went ahead and started eviction proceedings. They sent me a certified letter but I never got it. The complex would sign for packages or mail for the residents and they signed for the letter when I wasn't home to receive it. The manager told the girl that signed for it that she couldn't do that since the letter was from them. They returned it to the mailman nearly a week after they signed for it and I had a notice in my mailbox to go to the post office to pick it up. Of course, by the time I was notified of letter, the deadline for disputing the eviction in court had already passed. Since I didn't show up to dispute it, they awarded the eviction."

"That's bullshit! How could they get away with that?"

"I tried to work out something with the manager, but they had already changed the locks and she just wouldn't budge. The kicker was, they didn't even evict me for unpaid rent – the rent was paid. They did it over the late fees the manager charged me when I paid the September rent after the first. It was a good lesson in making sure arrangements like that are always in writing. Even if I had been able to dispute it in court, it was my word against theirs that a mutual agreement had previously been made."

"So, what did you do?"

"Hank offered to have us move in with him and his brother until I could get back on my feet. I moved in with them and let Emma stay with a friend for a while. She was fifteen at the time and Hank's was the ultimate bachelor pad and definitely not the place for a teenage girl."

"Well, that certainly sucks, but that wasn't necessarily a decision you made," Marie replied.

"Okay, there was the time I met a guy at the bar and invited him back to my place."

"You? I wouldn't have thought you'd be the kind of person to pick up some random guy at a bar."

"Emma was still pretty young. She was at my parents' for the night and I decided to go out. I was pretty lonely and got a bit too tipsy that night. I can't even tell you what his name was. Really, the only thing I remember is waking up in the middle of the night to see this stranger peeing in the corner of my bedroom."

Marie erupted with a guttural laugh. "What did you do?"

"I picked up his clothes and threw them at him and screamed for him to get the hell out of my house. The poor guy barely had his pants on as I pushed him out of the door. I have no idea what happened to him and, frankly, I don't care."

Marie had been at Julia's for several years and she had become restless. For weeks she tried to find the right time to tell Julia she had decided it was time to move on. They had become such close friends and Marie knew she would miss the old lady. One morning, as the two of them were preparing to open the store, Julia confronted the younger woman.

"How long you gonna dance around whatever it is you want to tell me?" Julia asked.

For a moment, Marie was stupefied but soon relaxed and grinned at Julia. "How the hell do you always seem to know what I'm thinking?"

"I've been around forever and you're not as mysterious as you think you are," she replied with a smirk.

Marie said, "I think it's time for me to go."

"Bout damn time! I was beginning to think you'd *never* get out of my hair," Julia teased.

"You got everything?" Julia asked.

"I think so.  I guess there really isn't much to get."

"Well, as soon as you get settled, I'll send the rest of your things."

"Julia, I want to..." Marie began.

"I know, sweetie, you don't have to say anything."

"Yes, I do. You have no idea just how much your friendship has meant to me these past few years.  I was such a mess a when I first walked into your store.  I still don't know how you did it, but you knew I was a wreck and you knew just what to say and do."

"You've come a long way since that scared little rabbit I first saw."

"Rabbit?"

"Didn't I ever tell you that?  That first day when you walked into the store, I instantly had the image of a rabbit frozen in fright with its little heart pounding away in its chest.  Your face showed just how defeated you felt, and your eyes showed you felt so lost.  I knew right away you had been running from something and that you just lost all of your energy and were giving up."

Tears filled Marie's eyes and she reached her arms out and hugged Julia tightly.

"I'll call you when I get there."

"Be careful."

# Even Adventures Must End Some Time

Locking up the store one evening Julia felt a strong sense of calmness wash over her. She looked out the window and peered around the stained glass of the tawdry saloon girl. The lights in the store were just bright enough for the colors of the artwork to be dimly reflected on the sidewalk outside. Stepping back slightly, Julia looked up toward the girl's face. The color of her once-vibrant red lips was muted and the dark-as-blood red dress appeared almost black against the darkened sky outside. The green of the plume in her hair was just barely visible. She stepped away from the window and looked around the store. Her gaze fell upon the wall of photographs. Her life was not always easy, but it was full of happiness and she had few regrets. Standing alone in the dark, Julia was flooded by memories of her beloved Hank.

*Neither Julia nor Hank realize at the beginning of the day that tonight will be the start of their long lives together. After dinner and karaoke, Julia takes Hank home. When she pulls into his driveway, he asks if she would like to come in for a little while. They get some beer from the refrigerator and take it into Hank's bedroom. He sits at the desk and loads CDs into the stereo. With no other chairs in the room, Julia must sit on the edge of the bed. As the music starts, Hank turns the chair to face her. They idly chat for a short time, then Hank leans in to kiss her. The first kiss is hesitant. Hank breaks away and looks into her eyes trying to get some direction as to how far he can go. Julia leans forward and, reaching behind Hank, places her beer on the desk. As she sits back down, she raises one hand slowly to his face. Hank slides closer to her and kisses her again, this time with more force. Soon, they are naked and entwined, kissing passionately and making love with greed.*

*Early the next morning, Julia awakens to find she is alone in the room. She can smell the rich aroma of strong coffee being brewed. She gets up and finds a T-shirt and some shorts in Hank's closet and puts them on. Quietly she leaves the room and walks to the kitchen. Hank is sitting at the table reading the paper.*

*"I hope you don't mind," Julia says as she shows off the outfit.*

*"I don't mind at all," Hank replies with a devilish grin.*

*They each pour a cup of coffee and walk out to the patio. Neither of them says anything for quite some time. The silence is not awkward but instead feels comfortable. Julia decides to ask what she knows he is thinking too.*

*"So, what do we do now?"*

*The two have become such close friends, it is easy to honestly talk about the fact this might be a one-night stand.*

*"I don't know," Hank replies. "I guess we can just see where it goes."*

Having returned to the present, Julia walked back to the large window.

Drawing the shade closed, Julia could just make out the shape of the girl cast by the street lights outside. Speaking to the shadowy figure, Julia said, "Goodnight you old broad you. Don't you go runnin' off to the dance hall, I need you to mind the store while I catch some shut-eye."

Walking to the back of the store, Julia was taken back to the past again as she remembered the first time she said those three little words to Hank.

*After a night of intensely passionate love-making, Julia and Hank are lying in the dark listening to the music paying softly. They are exhausted and sleep will fall upon them soon. As their breathing slows, Julia whispers, "I love you." She does not expect him to say anything. She knows it is probably too soon. Just as the thought enters her mind, he rolls over, kisses her lightly and replies "I love you too." Although she would not have thought it possible to have any strength left, the two make love again. This time, however, it is slow and tender.*

Ascending the stairs up to her apartment, Julia felt unusually relaxed. Climbing into the bed, she snuggled down into the covers and pulled the extra pillow close to her. Just as she drifted off to sleep, she murmured Hank's name.

"Ain't you done yet?" Hank asked.

"I'm comin', just hold on and don't get your panties in a twist," Julia replied.

She felt as though she laid down just a few moments ago but suddenly found herself standing at the bedroom window deep in thought. She felt Hank's arms wrap around her. She reached up to put her hand on his arm and noticed how young her hand looked.

"Bout time," he whispered.

"Hey Babe," she whispered back.

In unison, they asked each other, "It is Babe, isn't it?"

# PART 2

# The World Keeps Turning And Life Goes On

In the years since Marie moved away from Payson, she and Julia kept in touch.  There were occasional phone calls, but most of their corresponding took place in letters and cards.  Marie checked her mail one afternoon to find that a card she sent to Julia was returned as undeliverable.  Confused, Marie called Julia but the phone number had been disconnected.  Marie had no way to get in touch with any of Julia's family, but she did find one of the customers that frequented the store.

"Hi Frank.  I don't know if you remember me but, my name is Marie and I used to work at Julia's store."

"Hi Marie, of course I remember you.  How have you been?"

"I've been great.  I'm calling because a card I mailed to Julia came back and her phone number has been disconnected."

"Oh, sweetie, I'm sorry to be the one to tell you, Julia passed away a few months ago."

Marie sat in silence as the tears welled up in her eyes.

"You okay there?" Frank asked.

"I'm... I'm here.  I guess I knew this day would come, but it just seemed like she would always be there."

"I know what you mean.  We thought she'd outlive us all."

"Thank you, Frank."

"I'd say it was my pleasure but..."

"I know.  You take care of yourself, Frank."

"You too, miss."

Marie hung up the phone and sat quietly for quite some time.  The memories of her time with Julia flooded back and the tears began to flow down her cheeks.

Marie approached the store. The stained-glass woman does not reflect the colors onto her face this time. The store front was boarded up and the once magnificent door was cracked and faded. The for-sale sign tacked to one of the window boards was cracked with age and the realtor's information was just barely legible. Marie reached out to trace the lettering with her finger.

"Ma'am," a man said, startling Marie, bringing her out of her thoughts. "Sorry ma'am, I didn't mean to scare you," he said quickly.

"You're fine, Mr. Grady. Sorry, lost in thought I suppose," Marie replied.

The older man reached in his pocket and pulled out a ring of keys and approached the door.

"It's likely pretty dusty in there. I'm not sure when someone cleaned it last," he said with a shake of his head. "Oh, and please, call me Jack."

Leaving the door open to allow as much light as possible, Jack led the way into the store. Having been closed for quite a few years, there were cobwebs covering most of the shelves and the floor was covered in dust. Marie tried to ignore the tiny tracks in the dust. She already knew cleaning and getting the building restored was going to be a lot of hard work.

Marie made her way through the store and opened the door leading to the garden. Once vibrant and thriving, everything was shriveled and decayed. The brittle grape vines were intertwined with weeds. The many flower bushes were nothing more than tinder awaiting a spark to ignite a mighty bonfire.

"She loved this garden," Marie whispered.

As she turned to walk back into the building, a tiny sliver of color caught her eye. Near the center of the garden, just behind the chair where Julia sat day after day, a single rose had survived and had opened itself to receive the morning sun. With the faintest of smiles and a tiny tear escaping her eye, Marie went back into the store.

Jack Grady walked over to the counter and Marie was taken aback when her memory suddenly flashed to the scene when she first walked into the store so many years ago.

Having retrieved her suitcase and watching the bus drive away, Marie stands at the curb looking around at what appears to be the central are of the small town. She knows no one here and has no idea what to do next. Glancing across the street she sees what looks to be a bar but the sign says, 'General Store.'

She steps into the street and crosses without first looking for traffic. Her head is down and her hair has fallen into her face. As she reaches the sidewalk, she stands there momentarily lost as to what she should do next. The bright sun is reflecting off the ornate stained-glass window and the myriad of sparkling colors cover her face. Placing her suitcase on the bench outside the store, she reaches into the bag hung on her shoulder and pulls out an old handkerchief and uses it to wipe the tears from her face. She picks up her suitcase, inhales deeply and walks to the heavy oak door.

"Can I help you find something, miss?" an old woman stocking shelves asks.

The girl is somewhat startled, having missed seeing the woman while her eyes were adjusting from the bright sun outside. "Uh, um, no, I'm' fine," she barely whispers as she places her suitcase by the door.

"I'm guessing that's not entirely true, child. My name is Julia. If you need anything just let me know."

'Ok, old lady, mind your own business' the girl thinks to herself. She wanders aimlessly throughout the store. She has no money and, although she considers slipping some of the canned goods into her bag, she cannot go through with it. 'Besides, the ol' biddy is probably watching every move I make.'

Marie asks the woman if she has a bathroom she can use and Julia directs her to the back of the store. She retrieves her suitcase then enters the tiny bathroom looking at her reflection in the mirror. She looks horrible. Her hair is a tangled mess. Her eyes are dark and puffy and her nose is pink. The weight of the last few days is trying to crush her and, although she tries her best to avoid them, the tears start streaming down her face.

There is a light tap on the door and the old woman asks, "You okay in there sweetie?"

*She grabs some tissue and uses it to dry her eyes and blow her nose. She splashes some water on her face and takes a deep breath. Opening the door slowly she sees that Julia is standing in the hallway. For a very brief moment she meets the older woman's gaze. It is just marginally noticeable, but she can see Julia take a quick breath as she seems to back away ever so slightly.*

*As she makes her way up one of the aisles, she can hear to old woman's feet sliding along the old floor going toward the front counter. Lost in her own thoughts she realizes the woman has just asked her a question. Seeing that the woman has poured two drinks and placed them on the counter, the girl walks toward the front of the store and sits down on one of the bar stools. The woman comes around from behind the counter and sits on the stool next to the girl.*

*"First of all, what's your name?" Julia asks.*

*"Marie."*

*Again, distracted by her own wandering mind and staring into the soda in front of her, the girl realizes she is missing what the woman is saying.*

*"... a couple of things while we sit here."*

*The girl glances up slightly but looks back down as the woman continues talking and the girl catches, "he isn't worth all of this grief." Jerking her head up she stares into the face of the woman as the tears begin to flood her eyes.*

Using a handkerchief pulled from his pocket, Mr. Grady wiped off a spot on the counter. He reached into his briefcase and withdrew a stack of papers with colorful tabs sticking out of the bottom.

"Shall we get through the formalities first?" he asked.

Marie pulled up the rickety stool beside him, sat down and drew in a deep breath.

With a smile, she said, "Let's do this."

"Mommy, who's that man staring at us?" the little girl asked.

Marie turned quickly to look in the direction her daughter was pointing, just as the man began to cross the street toward them. A small grin crossed Marie's face when she recognized him.

Just before he reached the sidewalk, he asked, "Dropped any boxes on anyone lately?"

"Not yet, but now that *you're* here..."

Marie reached to give him a hug but nearly stumbled because her daughter was behind her, arms clamped around Marie's legs.

The man stopped, knelt and asked, "Who is this lovely young lady?"

Marie managed to break free of the death-grip and gently pushed her daughter a step toward the stranger.

"This is Amanda."

Marie squatted down so that they were all at eye-level and said to her daughter, "This is my friend Jason. His grandmother used to own the store."

"Mommy bought your JuJu's store," Amanda stated with strong will and determination in her voice.

Jason looked to Marie and said, "I knew the new owner was getting the store cleaned up, but I didn't know that was you. What'd you do? Win the lottery?"

Marie grinned and replied, "No. Ever heard of the book 'An Old Woman's Tales'?"

"I've heard my friends' wives talking about it." His eyes widened suddenly. "Wait, you?"

"Yes, me. You should read it, although you probably know it by heart. You've heard the stories all your life."

Jason came by often, pretending to offer his assistance getting the store ready but Marie knew his true intentions. They spent most of the time in the small backyard talking and watching Amanda play.

One evening, after Amanda was tucked into bed, the two went to the garden. The stars were exceptionally bright and the moon provided just enough light to see each other.

Marie walked up to Jason and said, "Julia taught me to let things happen naturally, not to force it. But she also taught me to go after what I want." Taking the glass of wine out of Jason's hand and slowly stepping toward him, she said, "I've been patient enough," and leaned into him for a kiss.

She had been afraid she might have been wrong and that he didn't feel the same toward her but those fears were dispelled when he quickly responded and urgently returned the kiss.

The days were spent cleaning up the long-neglected store. With Jason's help, Marie made simple repairs and replaced many of the store's broken and outdated fixtures.

Jason spent most of one afternoon repairing a wall in the store. Once finished, he stepped back to survey the result.

Dissatisfied, he exclaimed, "That's just shoddy."

Amanda stood behind him and assertively spoke. "Shoddy. S-h-o-d-d-y. Shoddy. Of inferior quality; hastily or poorly done. Shoddy."

For a moment Jason and Marie stood staring at the little girl. In unison, unable to hold it in any longer, laughter burst from each of them.

Grinning widely, Amanda asked, "What?"

"Where did that come from?" Marie asked.

Beaming with pride, Amanda answered, "It was one of my vocabulary words in school this week."

Their evenings were spent quietly with each other and, although she did not initially seem sure about the new man in her mother's life, Amanda began to accept Jason and grew to love him deeply. Each night Marie and Jason sat in the small garden behind the store, listening to music and talking.

"What made you want to buy the store?" Jason asked one night.

"The day I met Julia was a turning point for me. Even though I had some difficult times after I left here, I never forgot the stories she told me. Whenever I wanted to give up, I just reminded myself of some of the obstacles she had to overcome."

"So, you made a life-altering decision because of an old woman's stories?"

"In a manner of speaking, yes."

"You know, JuJu was always willing to share stories about herself but she never told me much about you. How'd you end up here?"

"In the words of your grandmother, Honey, I didn't *end up* here," Marie replied.

Grinning widely, Marie said "Well, I lived in this small town. It was quite boring but then one day this boy moved into the neighborhood. He wasn't like the rest of us. I guess you could say he was rebellious. Anyway, we weren't allowed to have school dances but he encouraged a bunch of us to go up against the town council..."

"You dork," Jason cut in. "That's a movie."

"Hmm. So, it is," Marie replied sheepishly. "How about this one then. I got in trouble at school one day, I don't remember for what, and I got detention. There were five of us at the school that day and the teacher kept leaving the room so, of course, we goofed off while he was away. We were all strangers before that day but we started to get to know each other and by the time we went home we were all friends."

"You know, you could just say you don't want to talk about it," Jason huffed.

"What? You don't believe me?"

Cutting his eyes toward her and, seeing the mischievous expression on Marie's face, Jason calmed a bit and teased, "Let me guess, you ended up with the bad boy."

"It's like you don't know me at all!" Marie quipped. "The jock was more to my liking."

Jason watched the silly grin on Marie's face slowly evolve to a look of concentration.

"You asked why I decided to buy the store. A few months before Julia died, an awful thing happened that changed me forever. I needed a fresh start; a place to escape. When I found out Julia passed away, I couldn't think of anywhere else I wanted to be. I also couldn't stand the thought of someone else running the store and not keeping her memory alive in this place. So, one morning I decided it was time to stop wishing I was here and do something about it. I made a few phone calls and found out the store was still for sale and here I am.

"What horrible thing happened?" Jason asked.

"911. What is your emergency?"

"Help me please! Send the police! Hurry!" Marie yelled frantically.

Marie watched from her window as the cruisers began to arrive and the police entered the neighbor's house. One officer knocked on Marie's door and asked her to remain inside until the investigators came to take her statement.

"I know this is hard for you," one of the detectives began, "just start from the beginning."

"Cynthia asked me to watch her dog and keep an eye on her house while she was out of town this week. She brought the dog over on Sunday night because she was going to leave very early Monday morning," Marie began. "When I got home from work tonight, I went over to her house to water the plants." Marie then recounted the events of that night.

She arrived home, let the dog outside then went to her room to change clothes. She was exhausted. It had been a tough day at work and she was glad Amanda was spending the night with a friend. She decided to go to Cynthia's house to water the plants then come home and sit mindlessly watching television until she fell asleep.

She arrived at the neighbor's house and opened the door. Immediately she smelled one of the vilest odors she had ever encountered. Thinking Cynthia forgot to take out the trash before she left, Marie walked to the kitchen intending to empty the garbage. The smell grew more intense as she approached the kitchen and she had to pull her shirt up over her mouth and nose. Upon entering the room, she discovered the window of the back door was broken and the door was not completely closed. Momentarily forgetting the stench, she stood frozen. Realizing she needed to get out of the house and call the police, she turned to leave. As she did, something in the adjacent dining room caught her eye. What she saw did not initially register and she was unable to recall later how long she stood there staring. Suddenly everything came together and Marie sprinted from the house. She tripped descending the steps from the front porch and landed hard on her knees. Scrambling back to her feet, she ran as fast as she was able and burst through the door of her own home. Shaking uncontrollably, she somehow managed to dial the phone.

"She was dead, wasn't she?" Jason asked.

She wiped the tears from her face and quietly answered, "Yes. She'd been stabbed in the face and chest and her throat was cut. There was so much blood. Her face was nearly obliterated from all the wounds and her blouse was shredded. They said they were able to determine she'd been dead since Monday morning. As horrifying as it was to find her that way, it was somehow made worse by the fact that Amanda and I had been walking her dog by her house and checking her mail for four days while she was lying there."

"Did they ever find out who did it?"

"Yes. It was the driver that had come to pick her up to take her to the airport. I never did hear whether or not he said why he'd done it. I didn't watch the local news after that day. I remembered it all too vividly and couldn't get it out of my head. The last thing I needed was some reporter rehashing it night after night. I had nightmares about it for a very long time."

"Do you still have the nightmares?"

"No," she replied. She then smiled slightly and her face relaxed. "Those stopped suddenly. I remember very well the first night I didn't have one."

Jason looked at her quizzically.

"The night I made the decision to move here and buy the store."

# Once Upon A Time

"So... I know Julia was your inspiration for writing the book, but what made you decide to actually start writing it?" Jason inquired one evening as he and Marie were sitting in the backyard.

Without saying a word, Marie got up and walked into the house. Confused, Jason sat there wondering what he had done wrong. Marie had never indicated there was anything about writing the book that would be painful, or something she did not want to discuss. Jason stood up intending to follow Marie to ask if she was okay, but when he turned toward the house, he saw Marie coming back with something in her hand.

Seeing the bewildered look in Jason's eyes, Marie explained. "I'll tell you, but I thought it would be better to show you too." She handed Jason the thick book. "Soon after I met Julia, she gave me this book. It had been her journal. She had removed all her written pages and replaced them with blank paper. Her father made it for her."

Looking down at the book, Jason ran his hand gently over the cover. He was awestruck as he realized he was holding something made by his great-grandfather. It was made of rawhide and had obviously been well used. The hide had developed a glossy sheen and the leather was buttery soft. The book was held closed by a thin ribbon that was new and provided quite a contrast against the ancient looking cover. He wondered how many times that ribbon had been replaced over the years. Carefully untying the ribbon, he slowly opened the book to find hundreds of pages with Marie's delicate handwriting. The two sat down and Marie told him of the day she began writing "An Old Woman's Tales."

She needed a break. She loved her daughter but the stress of being a single mother was taking its toll and she needed a day to herself. Amanda would be going home with a friend after school and Marie decided to call out of work. After dropping Amanda off at school, Marie returned home intending to lie around in her pajamas all day watching old movies or reading a book. She watched a movie but began to get restless. The six cups of coffee she consumed throughout the morning only intensified the feeling. She showered quickly and left the house with no plan of where to go. Too jittery to drive, she decided to walk and headed toward the shopping center a few blocks away. As she neared the shops, she began smelling the heavenly aroma from the tiny pizza

restaurant. Until that moment, she had not realized just how hungry she was, and she made her way to the entrance. Opening the door, she thought 'there aren't any smells quite as distinctive as those from a good ol' mom-and-pop pizzeria.' Because the restaurant was in a primarily residential area, it did not see an abundance of lunch traffic and most of the tables were empty. Marie chose a small booth in the corner where there was plenty of sunlight coming through the window. Soon after she sat down, a large man wearing a well-used apron approached, handed her a single-sided menu and asked if she would like something to drink. She asked for some water and a glass of white wine. He returned moments later and placed the drinks on the table.

"We don't have a server during the day so just holler when you're ready to order," he said in a rich baritone voice.

Marie thanked him and pulled the worn book from her satchel. She brought the journal with her with plans to write but the ribbon that kept it closed was in a knot. As she struggled to get the ribbon untied, the man returned to the table. He held a scissor in one hand and a length of ribbon in the other.

"We give out balloons to the kids and have a ton of ribbon in the back," he said as he handed her the items.

She carefully cut the old one and threaded the new ribbon into place. She ordered her lunch and when he walked away, she opened the journal. She flipped to the back and realized she had already used the last page. She pulled a few napkins from the dispenser on the table and started jotting down her thoughts. Lost in concentration, she was not aware the man had returned and cleared his throat to get her attention. She jumped slightly and blushed in embarrassment. He placed the food onto the table and asked if she would like another wine. She said she would and he left to retrieve it. When he returned, he had with him several sheets of paper.

"Thought you might like something better than napkins to write on," he said.

Marie graciously accepted the paper and, as he again left her table, she thought how kind and attentive he was. She ate slowly and continued to write. When she reached the bottom of the paper, she turned it over to use the back. What she saw made her grin. The paper he had given her was a stack of child's coloring placemats. She wondered how many of her journal entries had

been made on napkins, sticky notes and random scraps of paper. She turned to the beginning and began slowly flipping through the pages. The earlier entries had been made when she was living with Julia and, as she scanned the pages, a story started to form in her mind. Pulling a new sheet of paper from the stack, she began writing. She was soon engrossed and barely noticed when the man came to clear her dishes and fill the now-empty wine glass. When she ran out of paper, she returned to writing on napkins. One after the other, she filled the napkins with her feverish writing. She lost all sense of time and her surroundings as the story poured from her pen. It was not until an annoying sound penetrated her thoughts that she realized the pizzeria was filling up and kids were playing the various video games in the corner. Her thoughts returned to the present and she noticed she had nearly covered the table with her napkin scribbling. Only then did she glance at her watch and notice she had been writing for hours. She waved down the server who had come on duty and asked for her check. Marie carefully gathered the pieces of paper and placed them into the journal. She left the restaurant and was amazed to see that the sky was already turning shades of pink and orange as the sun began its descent.

The months went by quickly. Marie's and Jason's hard work was at an end and the store would be opening for business in a few days. The two sat in the now flourishing garden and enjoyed the cool evening.

"You talk about your time with JuJu easily but you don't talk much about between then and now. Why is that?" Jason asked one night.

"I had some rough years after I left here. I never told Julia much about it because I wanted her to think I was doing well, but it got pretty shitty for a while. You don't really want to hear about all of that do you?"

"As a matter of fact, I do. All of it. Even the shitty stuff."

"Hello?" the woman answered.

"Hey Mom. It's me," Marie said softly.

"What's wrong?"

"Can't I just call to say hi?" Marie responded defensively.

"Yes. But that's not the case, is it? I can tell something's up," her mother said.

"I want to... I need to come home," she blurted out just as the tears began.

For several minutes, the only sounds were those of Marie's sobs.

"He left me, Mom. We had a huge fight and he walked out. That was a week ago and I haven't heard anything from him. I called a few of his friends and they all said they hadn't seen him either. I'm pretty sure a couple of them were lying. He took the car and all his clothes. He just left us stranded here."

"Let me make some calls and call you back."

"I'm calling from a pay phone. I don't know what the number is, there's nothing on here."

"Alright. Um, call me back in a couple of hours. I'll see what I can do."

When Marie called later that afternoon her mother let her know a ticket was waiting at the bus station.

"Thanks, Mom."

"Uh huh. You actually need to thank your grandmother, she's the one paying for it."

"Not just for the ticket. Thanks for not saying it."

"Saying what?"

"I told you so."

Marie made as many peanut butter and jelly sandwiches as she could using the last of the stale bread. She counted the change from the jar. $3.80. In disbelief, she sat at the kitchen table and stared at the pile of coins in front of her and wondered just how it was that her life had been reduced to this. She had no idea how long she had been sitting there but came back to the present when the baby cried. She walked to the adjacent room and picked up Amanda. She rocked the baby in her arms and whispered over and over, "I'm so sorry." She looked at the clock and saw it was almost time for her friend to arrive to give her a ride to the bus station. She rechecked to make sure she had everything. She felt she had reached the lowest point in her life but was unaware of just how much worse things would get in the next few days.

She arrived at the bus station with her tiny daughter, a diaper bag and everything she owned ion two suitcases, Marie stood at the ticket counter where the attendant informed her that she could only take one of the suitcases. At a loss as to what to do she tried to plead with the clerk to allow her to take all of her belongings. Left with no other choice, she took some of the clothing from one bag and stuffed it into the other. The friend that gave her a ride promised to have the suitcase shipped. Reluctantly, Marie boarded the bus with only half of what she owned. After what appeared to be a rather long period of time, the driver closed the doors and started the engine. As the bus pulled out of the terminal, Marie was aghast when the driver announced to the passengers that they would need to let down all the windows because the air conditioner was not working. It was August and the temperature outside was over 100 degrees.

On the road, she watched Amanda sleep and recalled Julia's story of leaving Phoenix to return to Atlanta while pregnant with Emma. It was in that moment that Marie vowed she would never be this destitute again. From that day forward, she would feed upon Julia's stories of resolve and determination and would fight the be strong and independent.

Sweat trickled down Marie's neck and she reached over to feel Amanda's skin to make sure she was not getting too warm. She had been fanning the baby using the cardboard support from the bottom of the diaper bag and her arm was growing weak from the effort. The hot wind coming in from the windows helped dry the sweat but did nothing to cool the increasingly uncomfortable passengers. They had been riding for several hours and all on the bus had grown more and more restless and were beginning to vocalized their dissatisfaction to the driver. At the first extended

stop several of the passengers de-boarded and did not return. Marie assumed they had obtained seats on alternate routes but she had no choice but to remain on the bus and tried to settle in for the next leg of the trip. Soon after the bus returned to the highway, Amanda spit up and Marie took her out of the carrier. Holding the baby on her lap she began trying to clean up the mess. She was wiping off the baby's chin when the little one gagged slightly. Marie patted her gently on the back and the baby vomited. It covered not only the entire front of Amanda but was also down the front of Marie's shirt and into her lap. Marie quickly gathered the child and walked to the back of the bus to the bathroom. As she passed other passengers along the aisle, she could hear a few gags from the sight and smell. Marie herself was using all of her willpower to keep from being sick and was thankful when she made it into the bathroom and locked the door before she began to gag. There were several changes of clothes for the baby in the diaper bag but all of Marie's clothes were in the suitcase in the baggage compartment under the bus. She did her best to clean herself using a thick handful of wet paper towels and took both wet and dry towels back to her seat to clean up any mess there. Marie was thankful when, a few minutes later, Amanda drifted off to sleep. The child's seemingly peaceful slumber was violently interrupted a short time later when she suddenly threw up again. Again, Marie took the baby back to the bathroom and did her best to clean up. When she returned to her seat again, she noticed the various looks she was getting from the other passengers. While some were gazing upon the young mother and child with pity, many others were glaring with disgust. Feeling humiliated and angry over her current situation, Marie gathered her things and moved to an open row of seats toward the back of the bus so that she would not need to traverse the walkway in front of the strangers.

Once Amanda was again settled and sleeping, Marie took the baby's soiled clothes into the bathroom and washed them as best as she could. She draped the tiny shirts and pants over the arms of the adjacent seat to allow them to dry. She then returned to the bathroom to wash the bottles and it was then that she realized the heat inside the bus had spoiled the formula. Sitting in the seat next to the sleeping child, Marie began to cry and the feelings of hopelessness washed over her in waves. Night began to fall so the bus was finally cooling off a bit and before long Marie cried herself to sleep.

Just before dawn the next morning, the bus pulled into a station and the driver announced that they would have a one-hour wait.

Marie asked the driver if it would be possible to get to her suitcase so that she could get a change of clothes. It was obvious that the man did not want to do it but he eventually obliged since the compartment would be open for new passengers to load their belongings. Marie knew that the primary reason the driver gave this allowance was because she stunk and the passengers complained. She took the bag into the bathroom and changed her shirt and shorts. She then stole a garbage bag from the bottom of the trashcan and stuffed her dirty clothes into it. Before returning to the bus, Marie went to the small diner next to the bus stop and asked if they had anything she could use to help keep the remaining can of formula cool. The waitress said she might have something and disappeared to the back. She soon emerged with a small Styrofoam cooler and went behind the counter to partially fill it with ice.

Much of that day's ride was uneventful and Marie was able to relax a little and forget about the previous day. As noon approached, she could feel the increasing temperature inside the bus but it did not appear it would be as hot as before.

Early in the afternoon Marie decided to attempt to give Amanda some of the formula, hoping that the other one only spoiled because it had already been opened. Up until then, she had only been giving the baby water and so far, everything seemed to be staying down. All appeared to be going well until a few hours later when Amanda again got sick. This time however, the infant was not only vomiting but had diarrhea as well. Marie dealt with everything as best she could and kept reminding herself that they would be home tomorrow and this would be over.

That night however, when the bus pulled into Dallas, Marie was horrified to learn that it would be another two days before they reached the destination in Mississippi. When the trip began, Marie had not considered that a bus does not travel on a straight path, but rather zigzags to cover a larger area. Looking into the diaper bag, she counted only three more diapers. She obviously could not give Amanda any more of the formula and was afraid of what would happen if the baby had to live solely on water for too much longer. Frightened and on the verge of hysteria, she called her mother who calmed the girl down and told her not to worry. Her mother said she would contact the company and find out when the bus would arrive in Baton Rouge and would meet Marie there. With one crisis averted, Marie could further relax when she learned that they would be changing buses which meant they would have air conditioning. She was thankful when Amanda

made it through the night without being sick and both were able to get some much-needed rest.

The next morning, the bus again made an extended stop and Marie went into the tiny restaurant.  She ordered a soda and, much to the chagrin of the woman behind the counter, counted out the change consisting primarily of pennies.  Sitting quietly in one of the booths, Marie pulled the last of her peanut butter and jelly sandwiches from her purse.  It had been smashed among the contents of her bag and the grape jelly had soaked through the bread.  Just as she began to take a bite, a woman Marie recognized from the bus placed a plate of eggs, sausage and toast on the table.  Marie looked confusedly up to the woman who simply said "It's ok.  Go ahead.  You need something besides that nasty looking thing."  Marie was embarrassed but did not want to offend the woman and, because she was much hungrier than the sandwich would satisfy, she reluctantly ate the food.  It was not until she was finished that she fully realized how hungry she had been.  With a full belly and the knowledge that they would be off of the bus for good later that afternoon, Marie got back on the bus and hoped that Amanda's stomach upset would remain at bay.

The bus finally arrived in Baton Rouge and Marie felt she had never in her life been so glad something was over.  As soon as she stepped from the bus, she saw her mother walking toward her with outstretched arms.

"You may not want to do that," Marie warned as her mother started to give her a hug.

"Oh, pish!  There's no way I'm going to see my grandbaby for the first time and not give her a hug," her mother replied.

Marie carried the diaper bag and baby carrier while her mother held Amanda and the two women waited for the baggage to be unloaded from the bus.  Marie grew more and more anxious as bag after bag was removed and she did not see her own.  Once the last suitcase was taken off, Marie just turned in disbelief and stared at her mother.  Marie questioned the driver and he told her she would need to go inside and talk to someone there.  She spoke to a woman at the desk then walked over to where her mother sat with Amanda.  She dropped into one of the seats feeling completely defeated.

"What?" her mother asked.

"Apparently, my suitcase wasn't transferred when I changed buses last night. They said they'll have to ship it to the station near us and I'll have to pick it up there. What the hell am I supposed to do? All of my clothes are in there. I only have the dirty ones in the diaper bag and what I'm wearing now."

"We'll figure out something. Guess you'll have to do a lot of laundry. Come on, let's go. The sooner we get back home, the sooner you can clean up."

They had just entered the highway when Marie's mother exclaimed, "Damn, you really do smell!" and rolled down all of the windows.

Although she rarely went out, Marie decided to go with a group of friends for New Year's Eve. They had been having a great time laughing and singing along with the music being played on the jukebox. It was crowded in the tiny bar and Marie decided to step outside for some fresh air. On her way to the door, a group of guys walked behind her. One of them reached out and grabbed her butt. She turned and glared but let it go for the time being. The man was obviously drunk and Marie was determined to not let him ruin her night. She had only been outside for a few minutes when she decided to go back into the bar. The offender and his friends walked back into the bar behind her and she could hear them making lewd remarks. She turned to them and walked up to the man that grabbed her.

"Don't you ever put your hands on me again!" she yelled.

"Oh, come on baby, it's okay. I was just playing around," the guy mumbled drunkenly.

He then attempted to put his arm around Marie's shoulders. She moved away and turned to face him. Before she even realized she was doing it, she reached up and grabbed the man's throat and dug her nails into his skin.

"I SAID DON'T EVER TOUCH ME AGAIN, ASSHOLE!"

Marie let go of his throat and turned to walk back to her friends. It was only then that she noticed a hush had fallen across the bar and many of the other customers were staring in amazement. Several months later she learned that the man had caused another altercation in the bar and had been banned from ever coming back.

It was late and Marie was exhausted. She and Amanda had been away from home all day and she was looking forward to falling into bed. As they neared the house, Marie slowed down to pull into the driveway. The headlights illuminated the front of the house, and Marie could immediately see that something was not right. She stopped suddenly as the lights shone on the front window. The screen was bent and was pulled away from the window. She quickly backed out of the driveway and drove down the street to the gas station on the corner where she called the police from the payphone. The operator said that the officers were on the way and asked Marie to meet them at the house. She pulled to the curb several houses away from her home and one of the officers walked over to speak with her. The policeman took her statement as the other officers surrounded the house with their guns drawn. The elderly woman that lived next door was notoriously nosey and came out to her front yard asking what was going on. The officer closest to the woman asked her to please go back inside.

"That's typical," Marie said to the officer.

"What's that?" he asked.

"You guys are surrounding my house with guns pointed and that old bitty has to get right in the middle of it."

Once they had determined there was no one hiding anywhere around the house, they came to get the keys from Marie so they could search inside. Marie was hesitant. She knew they needed to do their job and she wanted them to make sure there was no one inside, but she was embarrassed. She had been depressed lately and her housekeeping was non-existent. She was afraid they would take Amanda away from her once they saw the condition inside. If it had only been messy, she could have blamed it on whoever broke into the house, but there was trash everywhere. Empty soda cups and crumpled fast-food bags littered the floor. The kitchen sink was full of unwashed dishes, some of which had been there for weeks.

"It's gross in there," she said as she handed over the keys.

"I'm sure we've seen worse."

She was sure they had as well but it did nothing to quell her anxiety over what they would see as they made their way through the house. Within just a few minutes, the officers came out of the

house and Marie braced herself for what they would say. She was overwhelmed with relief when they handed her back her keys, told her it was safe to go into the house and left without saying anything about taking Amanda away.

Marie and Amanda stood on the porch talking with the babysitter. The little girl became restless listening to the grown-ups talk and wandered to the end of the porch. Marie watched as Amanda walked down the two steps and stood by the car. The women began talking again and Marie was lost in the conversation for a moment. She looked toward the car but did not see Amanda. She called the child's name but there was no answer. Almost as an afterthought, Marie looked down the driveway and her heart skipped a beat when she saw Amanda walking toward the street. Immediately, Marie remembered Julia's story of Emma nearly walking out into a busy street. She tried to keep calm but Amanda was already very close to the end of the driveway. Marie leapt from the porch and ran toward her daughter.

"Amanda! Stop!" she yelled.

The little girl just giggled and started to run. Marie was afraid she would not make it to the girl in time. She lunged forward and managed to grab a handful of the child's hair, yanking her down hard. The two fell to the gravel of the driveway, just as a car sped by on the street. Holding her daughter tightly, Marie rocked back and forth.

"Don't you ever run away from me again," she whispered to the little one in her lap.

"My promise, Mommy," Amanda replied through her tears.

The re-opening of the store brought a much-needed heart beat to the slow-moving town. The months went by and the little business thrived. Marie and Jason's relationship grew strong and they found a little house just outside of town. Just before Christmas, Jason proposed and Marie, of course said yes. The small family settled into a routine.

One morning, when they arrived to the store, Marie recalled again the first time she walked up to this place. She stood looking at the saloon girl in the window and smiled as a small tear ran down her cheek. Jason approached her gently put his arm around her waist. They stood silence, neither feeling the need to speak. They both knew the other was thinking of Julia and that it was a time for thoughts and emotion, not words. Deciding that Marie needed a moment alone to

gather herself, Jason walked toward the stained-glass window. The saloon girl had been refurbished and once again gleamed in the sunlight.

Amanda walked over and took her mother by the hand and began to walk toward the store. The two took a few steps and Amanda let go of Marie's hand and walked up to Jason who was wiping a dirt spot from the glass. Basking in the warm sunshine, Marie stood there and looked at Jason and Amanda as the sun reflected the colors over her face and her abdomen, which was just starting to show a little bump.

Caressing her stomach, Marie looked up to the skies and smiled. "Thank you, Julia. You were one helluva woman and you gave me so much."

Jason walked over to Marie and said, "A penny for your thoughts."

"Ha! These thoughts are priceless, you can keep your penny," Marie replied with a grin.

"Tell me," Jason pleaded.

"I can only hope that someday I'll be the kind of woman she became."

# Epilogue

The snow outside is finally letting up. Amanda checks the phone to see if service has been restored but the line is still dead. She and her brother have been at the cabin for several days but their parents' arrival has been delayed due to a storm. Internet service is still available so she searches for reports of road conditions in the area.

"It looks like they've cleared most of the roads," Amanda tells her brother.

"You know Dad has been trying to convince Mom the roads are fine," he replies.

"Of course," Amanda answers.

Just then, Amanda's cell phone rings.

"Hi, Mom."

Amanda looks at her brother, smiles and rolls her eyes.

"Okay, we'll see you soon," she says to Marie.

"They'll be here in about twenty minutes," Amanda tells her brother.


Marie and Jason arrive and the four of them unload the car. Once everything has been put away the family gather in the cozy living room.

"So, what did you two do to occupy the time with no working television?" Marie asks.

"Thanks a lot for not telling us about that by the way," Amanda says.

"Hey, I told you there were very few amenities up here. That's the very reason we love it. Besides, I doubt you would have been able to watch anything anyway – I'm sure the cable's out," Jason says.

"So, what'd you do?" Marie asks again.

"I've been telling him the stories of the two of you and JuJu," Amanda replies.

Julian turns to his parents and says with a laugh, "All I did was ask if she knew how I got my name.  That was three days ago and I swear she hasn't shut up since."

Made in the USA
San Bernardino, CA
11 April 2019